EMBERS FOR NONE

WHEN FLAMES NEVER LEARN WHO THEY ARE BURNING FOR.

ANISHA DUTTA

For Rikibiki, Pom Pom, Bobbie, and Mojo

The four souls who taught me what it means to be seen without words, to give without asking, to stay through storms, and to leave behind a love that never truly leaves.

You showed me how deep connections can go...Beyond language, beyond reason, into something quieter, vaster.

Not quite love as the world defines it...But something older. Truer. A soul-thread.

You taught me what selfless presence is. What parting feels like. What it means to carry someone in silence.

And even though you are not beside me, you are everywhere I go. In the stillness. In the light. In the way I love now.

This story is for you...

Because though you are gone, you are kind of forever.

You held my heart in your paws. And I am still learning how to walk without you.

Contents

Contents

Preface

Some stories do not come crashing in. They arrive slowly like the hush after rain, like breath fogging a window in winter. They do not belong to one person. They live in glimpses, in the way someone looks away too quickly, or clutches a keepsake a little too long.

This story came to me that way, simply from connecting with those who sit across from each other in cafes with eyes that say too much and mouths that say too little. From the ones who move through the world like something is missing, though they cannot name it. From the quiet ache between souls who clearly once belonged to each other—maybe still do—but life got in the way.

It was born from places that have no words—only shadows, only echoes. From the kind of connection that does not fit into the neat outlines of love or friendship or fate. Something older. Something deeper. A thread that tugs across lifetimes.

Some souls, I have come to believe, are meant to find each other. Not always to stay. Not always to be named. But simply to awaken something. To stir the dust in our bones. To remind us that we are not made for small feelings.

This book is also for the ones who walk beside each other without speaking, who know when to stay close and listen, asking for nothing but presence.

If you have ever watched someone walk away and felt like your ribs might collapse. If you have ever stayed up wondering what a connection could have been, had it arrived a moment sooner, or a lifetime later. If you have ever felt haunted in a way that had nothing to do with ghosts, but with twin fires that burn across miles, but still burn the same with fiery intensities.

Then maybe this story was always meant to find you.

I do not and cannot offer answers. Only this: Some bonds are not meant to be understood. Only felt. And remembered.

EPIGRAPH

For when silence grows too heavy, and the soul aches for something it cannot name.

One Word of Tenderness
"Sitting by the seashore
On an inky black sky
Studded with diamond stars shining down
And the empowering roar of the waves
Like the arms of a long-lost lover reaching out to you
And the tender wisps of wind kissing
The cascade of that beautiful hair
And the desperate loneliness
Creeping within that palpitating heart
Craving for one word of tenderness."
—Ann

Prologue

Sweet Scars of Torture

She wakes up, gasping.

The candle on her nightstand has melted into a deformed ruin. Smoke lingers in the air, like something holy has just left. Her nightgown clings to her spine, soaked. The room is still. Too still.

Another dream. Another ghost.

He visits her not in memory, but in marrow. In that place behind her ribs where logic loses its voice. Where the body remembers what the mind denies.

Tonight, she is standing at a riverbank again. He stands across the water—soaked, shivering, hollow-eyed. She screams his name, but no sound comes. And when she reaches for him, the river rises, takes her by the knees, the waist, the chest—and she drowns without dying.

There have been others. Dreams where he kissed her and her mouth bled. Dreams where she stabbed him, then wept over his body. Dreams where they danced—wild and unclothed—under the moonlight, until his flesh turned to ash in her arms.

Each dream, a parable of their passion. Each dream, a warning she never heeded.

There was a time she convinced herself it was just longing. Nostalgia, maybe. But today she knows, this is not longing. This is spiritual haunting. This is obsession with fingernails and teeth.

This is the sweet torture of knowing the one thing that ever felt like home was also the one thing she was too afraid to hold.

She betrayed it. Not with lies. Not with cruelty. But with silence in chaos. With pride and scorn. With the terror of being seen—and the greater terror of being known.

"Who are you that prowl in the murk?" She had written once in her diary. *"Lost in my heart, cavernous and dark."*

He was a ghost she invited. He was the wound she opened wider. The twisted knot between passion and destruction—she tied it herself.

She was the fire, and he the forest. And now, years later, she wanders the charred remains of what might have been.

She returns, again and again, to the place where she killed the love herself. With fear. With ego. With the cowardice of a girl who wanted love but not the cost of it.

She staggers to the mirror. The woman staring back is not the girl he loved. But the eyes—ah, the eyes still carry the ruins.

She lifts her nightgown slightly, tracing a line above her hip, where she once imagined his hands would rest if they had grown old together. The skin is unmarked. But something deeper aches.

"Why do I love you...and, why do you, too?" She had once asked the dark.

It never answered...only lingered.

He had loved her with the intensity of rain on a droughted field. She had feared the flood.

Now, she sleeps alone. She is calm. She is almost at peace.

But some nights...when the sky turns indigo and the earth begins to breathe, she hears the whisper of piano keys she never learned to play.

This is not heartbreak. Heartbreak passes. This stays. It coils behind her ribs. It lives in her pulse.

Leaving behind sweet scars of torture...and she will carry it, always.

I
Caramel Promises and Painted Dreams

Riversley belongs in a storybook—the kind with yellowing pages and fine ink sketches. Cobblestone lanes crisscross through rows of ivy-clad cottages, their chimneys always trailing soft ribbons of smoke. Tucked between rolling green hills and the hush of the slow-moving Caeldra River, this sleepy little town breathes in rhythms older than memory. Caeldra's waters glow silver at dawn, gold by dusk, winding their way past weeping willows and the occasional lost paper boat.

In the town's centre, stands the clock tower, watching over it all like a gentle, aging guardian. At first light, the scent of warm bread drifts from Madame Louis' Bakery and coils through the alleys. Across from it, the florist's stall bursts with wild lavender, butter-pale peonies, and bunches of rosemary strung with raffia. At The Wren & Quill Cafe, wicker chairs lean lazily into the sun, occupied by morning regulars murmuring over teacups and folded newspapers.

Just a short walk down Hollowmere Lane is St. Mary's Church, its stained-glass windows splashed with saints and sunrays, casting kaleidoscopic light on worn pews and hushed prayers. Bells toll softly at noon, a sound so familiar it no longer turns heads—just settles gently in the chest, like breath.

And tucked away between two old brick townhouses lies Calloway's Bookshop, a dusty haven where sunlight streams through arched windows and time forgets to move. It smells of parchment and pipe tobacco, and the floors creak like they are sharing secrets.

Further down, Wesley Lane curls into view, narrow and uneven, with crooked fences and children's bicycles left abandoned in haste. It is here that the ordinary days unfold—the ones stitched quietly with friendship, laughter, and the early blush of something that might one day be love.

Here, two houses sit across from each other like two versions of a story told differently.

The Marlowe house is orderly and soft-spoken. A rose-hued cottage with a periwinkle door and perfectly trimmed hedges, it seems to hold its breath in politeness. Lace curtains billow in the windows, and the flowerbeds are precise rows of marigolds and bluebells. Everything has its place. And so does Elise Marlowe, the girl who grows up inside it.

Elise moves with quiet grace. There is a stillness to her—composed, almost solemn—but in the tilt of her head or the arch of a brow, something untamed glimmers. She draws in the margins of her schoolbooks, paints imaginary buildings in impossible colours, and reads like she is gathering spells.

Her hair is a tumble of chestnut curls, usually tucked into a loose plait, and her fingers are often ink-stained from where she has pressed too hard on the page.

Across the lane, the Whitmore house leans slightly to one side, as though it is laughing at its own untidiness. The garden is wild with honeysuckle and daisies, and shoes lie abandoned on the porch next to a dented football. A piano tune sometimes drifts from the window—a delicate melody that slips into the air like a sigh.

Everyone knows the music belongs to the kind and charming Mr. Whitmore, owner of the only music shop in Riversley.

And the boy who lives there, Leo, is all elbows and soft brown wild hair, with a grin that looks like it is keeping secrets. He collects scraped knees, lost homework, and the quiet admiration of classmates without trying. He slouches in his chair just enough to make the teacher pause mid-sentence, fingers tapping a rhythm only he hears. He speaks when he feels like it, and when he does not, he smirks instead.

Leo and Elise attend St. Clement's Primary School. The building is old but proud, with blue shutters faded by time and tall windows that catch sunbeams and secrets alike. Inside, the air carries the soft dust of chalk, the faint sweetness of pencil shavings, and the rustle of paper that always sounds like it is trying to say something more.

Elise is seated across Leo in the farthest row of their 4B classroom. They have known each other since their first day at school, and of course, as neighbours. But it is only on that one remarkable Tuesday when they have their first proper exchange.

Leo slides a caramel sweet wrapped in gold foil across her desk without a word.

Elise blinks. Then she looks at him.

"For you," he says, like it is nothing.

She hesitates for half a second, then takes it. Their fingers brush. He grins—one dimple, like punctuation.

The next morning, another caramel appears on her desk.

And the morning after that.

It becomes a ritual—quiet, wordless. On days he forgets, Elise raises a brow and waits, pretending not to. He scrambles in his pockets, feigns surprise, and hands one over, even if it has slightly melted.

As the days pass, they begin to speak in glances. A smirk means *"Meet me after class."* A nudge of an elbow under the desk translates to *"Miss Holloway is watching."* Their friendship unfolds in scenes—short, unsaid, but full of colour.

Leo writes, though he does not tell many. Little stories. He jots them down in the corners of his notebooks, folds scraps into his pockets like treasure maps. Words, to him, are another kind of music. But he does not let people in—not fully.

Elise paints. Not flowers or bowls of fruit. She sketches soaring buildings with winding staircases, towers that touch clouds, doorways that look like they might open into other worlds. She never draws people.

"You never paint anyone," Leo says one day, chin resting on his palm as he watches.

"People never stay still long enough," she replies, not looking up.

"I would," he says.

She rolls her eyes, but something warm flickers in her chest.

Although they live across each other, it is not until they are eleven that Elise finds out...

One afternoon, after school, Leo calls out to her across the lane. "You want to come over?"

She blinks. "Now?"

"Yeah. I want to show you something."

Inside, the Whitmore house smells like cinnamon, lemon tea, and forgotten books. It is messy in a way that feels alive. There are mismatched cushions on the couch, doodles tacked to the fridge, a sock hanging inexplicably from the banister.

He leads her to the room at the back.

A piano stands by the window, sunlight glazing its polished surface. Leo does not say anything. He just sits down, places his fingers on the keys, and begins to play. The room hushes around them.

Elise stares, breath caught. She has heard this music before—soft and aching, threading through her evenings like a secret. But she had always thought it was Mr. Whitmore.

"You?" she says softly, when he finishes. He shrugs. "Yeah."

All at once, something shifts. She sees him not just as the boy who forgets his tie and scribbles comics in his homework, but as someone with corners she has not discovered yet. Someone with songs in his hands.

She sits beside him on the bench, their shoulders not quite touching.

"You're good," she murmurs.

Leo doesn't look at her, but he smiles.

II
The Sound of Distant Strings

By the time they start at Riversley High, the world stretches a little wider.

The buildings loom taller, the corridors echo longer, and the once-familiar rhythm of St. Clement's dissolves into a dozen ringing bells and shifting classrooms. Here, nothing stays still. Teachers rotate like clockwork, friendships shift with seating plans, and the air is thick with the unspoken pressure of becoming someone—fast.

Gone are the blue shutters and chalky warmth of their old school. Now there are science labs that smell of antiseptic and metal, lockers that stick, and stairs that feel endless. Even the sunlight feels different—colder somehow, sharper, as if watching closely.

But some things stay.

Leo still walks beside Elise, still tosses her a candy when no one is looking, and still grins like the world is his favourite inside joke. He adapts with frightening ease. By thirteen, he is the boy who leans against his locker with his tie half-undone, his shirt untucked, and piano books slung under his arm like an afterthought. The kind of boy who hums symphonies under his breath and does not care who hears.

People gravitate toward him without needing to be asked.

Elise watches from the sidelines, amused and unbothered. She knows the truth behind the easy charm—the way he still sits cross-legged at his piano at home, barefoot, shoulders hunched, lost in a melody he will never write down. She knows how his fingers twitch during maths class when a tune catches in his head. She knows him, even if the rest of the school only sees the silhouette.

She prefers the background anyway. Always has. Calm, poised, a little unreadable. People assume she is the quiet one, the sensible girl with neat handwriting and perfect grades.

They do not see the way her mind runs wild behind steady eyes. But someone does.

It begins with a letter.

Folded neatly, tucked between the pages of her history book. The handwriting is careful, like someone afraid of getting it wrong. She does not read it at first—just stares at it, fingers resting lightly on the paper as if it might vanish if touched.

That night, lying on her bed beneath the glow of her desk lamp, she unfolds the note.

"Dear Elise,

This is hard to write. Not because I do not know what I feel, but because I do not know if I have the right words for it. Still, I am going to try.

I think I am falling for you.

Not all at once, and not in any way that'is dramatic. Just slowly, like how the sky changes in the evening—quiet, almost unnoticed, until suddenly everything is golden and you do not remember how it began.

It is not just one thing. It is never just one thing with you.

It is the way you carry yourself—like you belong to some older, steadier world. But then your eyes give you away. I have seen them get livid when you are angry, or flare up when something excites you, and it is like something untamed comes through the calm. Like wind slipping through a closed window.

You always seem so composed, but I do not think it is the kind of quiet that comes from having nothing to say. I think you are full of things. Stories. Thoughts. Places you go to in your mind when the real world feels too small.

And Elise...

You are so cute and...pretty. Have you ever noticed?

You are beautiful, not the kind that asks for attention. The kind that stays in someone's mind long after they have stopped looking. You are gorgeous when you laugh at things no one else hears. When you stare out of windows like they might open onto somewhere new. When your hair falls into your eyes and you do not even notice.

I know I am not the person you probably expect this from. Maybe you do not even really see me. That is okay. I just wanted you to know—

Someone sees you. Not the quiet, neat version people think you are. But the version that draws impossible cities, and sometimes forgets to come back down to earth.

That version?

I think she is remarkable.

—Jamie"

Her breath catches.

No one has ever written to her like that. No one has ever looked past the surface long enough to notice the storm beneath.

She reads it again. Slower, this time. As if the words might shift if she blinks too fast.

The handwriting is neat but slightly slanted, like it rushed ahead of him, as if he had too much to say and was not sure how to contain it. She recognises it now—Jamie—the charming blonde boy from her form group who always lingers a second longer than necessary when he passes her, who once returned a sketchbook she did not even realise she had dropped.

She had never paid him much attention. Not because she did not see him, many girls did. She had not bothered because she assumed he never paid her any attention either.

But this letter...

It feels like someone has cracked open a window inside her.

That weekend, she stands in front of the mirror longer than usual.

She brushes a curl back, then lets it fall again.

There is a freckle just below her left brow that she has never really noticed before. Her collarbone catches the light, delicate but pronounced now. She shifts her shoulders and watches how her shape has changed—soft curves where once there was only straightness. Her waist, her hips, the growing hush of something womanly.

She tilts her head.

What does he see?

She has always felt like the quiet one. Not invisible, just...contained. But now, for the first time, she wonders if there is something more. Something others might notice—have noticed.

And though she does not mean to, a touch of vanity creeps in. Not the loud, showy kind. The quiet kind. The kind that settles in the corners of your smile.

She is not used to feeling beautiful.

But maybe she is.

Maybe, somehow, someone has seen her before she has even fully seen herself.

She shows Leo the letter on Monday.

He raises an eyebrow, reads it aloud in mock-theatrical horror, and clutches his chest like a wounded actor mid-tragedy. "I think I am falling for you...," he declares, voice dripping with drama. "You are so cute and...pretty..."

"Give it back," she laughs, smacking his arm. "Idiot."

He grins as he hands it over. "You are indeed cute when you blush."

She scoffs, but the corner of her mouth betrays her.

She is glowing in a way he has not seen before. Not just the way her eyes flicker when she is amused or how her hair catches the sun like a spill of ink, but something softer, deeper. A warmth blooming from within.

And unknown to him, or perhaps known all too well, Leo feels a pang.

It is not jealousy, not exactly. Not yet. It is more like displacement. Like watching someone reach for a story you thought you were still writing. He does not say anything, of course. He never does when it matters most.

And then, as if to prove it, the universe gives her Jamie Carter.

Jamie is charming in a different way—simple, steady, without effort or artifice. He has a slightly crooked smile and the habit of playing with his hair when he is nervous. He listens with real attentiveness, laughs without calculation, and walks beside her like it is the most natural thing in the world.

He remembers her favourite chocolates—the orange ones she pretends not to like but always eats first. He leaves silly sketches in the margins of her notebooks, inked with little arrows and notes like *"That's a spaceship, obviously."* He waits outside the gates when it rains, holding a shared umbrella, and walks her home when the sky turns gold with dusk.

They find secret places—beneath the old oak tree near the sports field, in the back aisles of libraries, behind the stone wall of St. Mary's Church—where they whisper about nothing and everything.

Jamie slips sweets into her pockets, just like Leo once did.

But they never taste quite the same.

Then, one afternoon, beneath the hush of that same old oak, Jamie leans in and kisses her.

It is soft...sweet...exactly the kind of kiss a thirteen-year-old girl dreams of.

And just at that exact same moment, Leo passes. Elise is immersed in her world and does not notice. He does not linger either—just a glance—a fleeting moment—and walks away, hands clenched at his sides, dark eyes unreadable.

The next afternoon, after the last bell, he finds her by the bike racks behind the school. There is a strange tightness in his posture—shoulders stiff, jaw set—and when he speaks, his voice is quieter than usual. Strained.

"The letter you got," he says, and his tone is taut as a piano string about to break. "I dictated it."

Elise blinks.
"What?"

"Jamie came to me," Leo goes on, his hands gesturing now, half-defensive, half-exhausted. "He wanted to impress you. And since I know you so well, I—"

Her stomach drops.
The world seems to tilt, just slightly.

"You helped him write it?" she asks, barely above a whisper.

"Yeah," he huffs, running a hand through his hair like it might calm something wild inside him. "And you—"

But she does not let him finish.

She rifles through her books and pulls the letter out, crumpled now from days of being folded and unfolded. She shoves it against his chest.

"Why would you do that?" Her voice is shaking now. "Why would you make me think—"

"You were going to date someone sooner or later," Leo mutters, looking anywhere but at her. "What does it matter?"

"It matters because it was supposed to be real," she says, softer now.
The anger in her tone thins, replaced by something far more dangerous—hurt.
"Because I liked believing it was real."

There is something flickering in his eyes—guilt, maybe. Or fear. Or something he does not yet know how to name.

But it vanishes as quickly as it appears.

"You are a hypocrite," Elise snaps, stepping back, voice rising again.

"You are dating Colette Hughes now, are not you? You flirt with every girl in school. But the moment someone else looks at me, you suddenly care?"

Leo's jaw tightens. His fists curl at his sides.

"It is not the same."

"You are right," she says bitterly. "Because I do not lie."

Leo opens his mouth—but no words come.

For the first time since she has known him, Leo is silent.

And just like that—

The fragile, golden thing between them shatters.

They stop speaking.

No more scraps of sweets left on her desk.

No more inside jokes scrawled in the margins of her notebooks.

For the first time since she was nine years old, Leo is no longer a part of her world.

And Elise?

She does not wait.

She walks past him in the corridors like he is no one.

She waves to Jamie when he catches her eye, lets him hold her hand at lunch, and laughs at his now-terrible jokes.

She watches from a distance as Leo leans against lockers, spins Colette in dizzy circles at the school disco, smiles too widely, and laughs too loudly.

She tells herself it does not hurt. She tells herself it never mattered as much as she thought.

But on nights when she walks by the river, when the wind is still and the stars blink softly above Riversely—she swears she can hear the faint, aching sound of a piano drifting through the trees.

And even though she tells herself not to—
She always listens.

III

You Will Always Be My Beatrice

The silence between them stretches for months.

At first, Elise thinks it will pass—that one of them will crack. Maybe he will find her in the library and slide a note across the table. Maybe she will glance at him in drama class and they will laugh about something ridiculous again. But time moves differently now.

They no longer orbit each other.

Instead, she walks beside Jamie Carter for a while.

He is sweet, steady, always waiting outside the art block with a snack in hand or a folded paper heart in his pocket. But sweetness starts to feel like weight.

Jamie wants more of her than she can give—text replies within minutes, shared breaks, public hand-holding, and an unspoken demand that she split herself in two just to keep him secure.

At first, she tries.

But the days begin to feel cluttered, like her mind has been scribbled over.

When she opens her sketchbook, the lines are messier.
When she studies, the pages blur.
When she wins a debate, she sees his sulk in the corner instead of pride.

And slowly, Jamie begins to irritate her in ways she cannot explain.

He does not understand silence.
Not the kind that feels whole.

At times, she recalls her afternoons with Leo.

The ease. The quiet.
The way theywould lie under the jacaranda tree near the library—he scribbling thoughts into his new leather-bound journal, her sketching something in her lap, books propped open on the grass.

Sometimes, they would not speak for an hour.
Then, as if pulled by the same invisible string, they would both blurt out something random—

"Do you think all stars make a sound?"

"What if people were colours?"

"What if shooting stars are fire-breathing dragons?"

"What if I am a witch?"

"No, you are an enchantress!"

And they would look at each other and laugh.
Like the world had written them into the same page before they even knew it.

Now, with Jamie, there is only noise.
And so, she begins to pull away.

At first, slowly—delayed replies, excuses, missed calls.
And then one Friday after school, she says the words.
"This is not working."

Jamie blinks. "Why not?"

She hesitates. She could say, "I need to focus on myself."
She could say, "It is not you."
But the truth, she realises, is harder to admit.

"Because I am not who I used to be."

And it is true.
She's growing in ways she had not imagined.

Her artwork is impeccable. Her pieces win awards.
She places top in debates.
Teachers call her name in assemblies.
Boys linger longer when she walks past.
Girls glance at her with a mixture of admiration and envy.

Her once-slender figure is now all grace and angles, sharp cheekbones, curves beneath crisp blazers. Her hair, always a little unruly, cascades past her shoulders like it has a mind of its own.

And sometimes, Elise stands in front of the mirror and sees someone beautiful. Someone powerful.

Sometimes, vanity whispers in her ear.

She considers walking up to Leo. Saying something. Anything.

But each time she gathers courage, she sees him—laughing with a new girl by the lockers, balancing a football on his foot during break, tapping out rhythms on the piano while a crowd hovers around.

It is not Colette anymore. It is someone else. It is always someone else.

He seems fine.
Untouched.

So she lets it be.
If he does not care, why should she?
But Leo is watching, too.
He watches as Elise walks through the corridors with her chin high, her words sharper than they used to be, her

sketches bolder.

He sees how she commands a room during debates—fiery, eyes flashing with certainty.

She does not need him anymore. Maybe she never did.

Still, something in her has shifted.

He sees her anger more often.

She snaps at groupmates. She sighs during discussions. She rolls her eyes with a new kind of edge.

And her silence toward him—it is not cold.

It is complete.

So Leo retreats.

He fills his hours with sport. With scripts. With music. His plays start gaining attention—monologues sharp and intimate, full of broken people saying the things no one ever says aloud. Teachers praise his emotional depth, his grasp of dialogue.

But what they do not know is—he rewrites voices and memories.

Of the people around him. Of girls lending him a piece of their heart. Of moments half-remembered.

But he never rewrites Elise. He considers her too special. The fragments of her, her scorn, her silences, her soft bewilderments—they appear only in his thoughts and will stay there, safe, untouched.

However, Elise knows where his scripts come from. She is the only one who notices that his enactments are too familiar.

A girl who hates compliments. A boy who ruins everything with pride. A friendship that falls apart over a misunderstanding.

And slowly, a thought creeps in. One day, will I become a subject to him as well? The notion stays with her, sticky and cruel.

So she decides, in that hasty manner she always does, that Leo can never be trusted with the parts of her that matter. She resolves it quietly, but completely.

If he ever wants back in.
He will have to fight for her trust, something he never broke, but in her tangled thoughts, he did.

Slowly, Autumn arrives, and with it, the school play. In Year 9, it is not compulsory, but those who want to be part of it stay after school for rehearsals. This year, the English department chooses 'Much Ado About Nothing'—a play about love, misunderstandings, and two people too stubborn to admit they care.

Mrs. Moreau, the drama teacher, announces the casting after the first round of readings.

"Leo Whitmore and Elise Marlowe will play Benedick and Beatrice."

Silence.

Elise's breath catches. Across the room, Leo stills.

They have not spoken in almost a year. Now, they are expected to perform together—to argue, to dance, to look at each other the way lovers in plays do.

Elise swallows. "Mrs. Moreau, I—"

"The decision is final," Mrs. Moreau says briskly, moving on.

And just like that, they are forced back into each other's orbit.

At first, they speak only when necessary.

Rehearsals are awkward. The words of Shakespeare's play—so full of wit and hidden longing—feel like sharp edges between them.

"You are supposed to look at me when you say that line," Leo mutters one afternoon, arms crossed.

Elise tightens her grip on her script. "I am."

"You are looking at the floor."

"Well, maybe the floor is more interesting."

Leo exhales sharply. "You are impossible."

Weeks pass. The tension softens, bit by bit.

One evening, as they rehearse in the dimly lit auditorium, something shifts. The scene demands a fight—Benedick and Beatrice, full of fire, throwing words like weapons. Elise throws herself into the role, her voice sharp, her eyes flashing.

"I wonder that you will still be talking, Signior Benedick: nobody marks you...."

Leo does not break character. "What, my dear Lady Disdain! Are you yet living?"

For a moment, the room stills.

Then—Elise smirks. "Bad luck, Whitmore. You are stuck with me."

Leo laughs, the sound unexpected and warm.

Something between them cracks open.

As the final rehearsals approach, the masquerade ball scene becomes a focus—Beatrice and Benedick, moving through the intricate steps of a dance, their sharp words at odds with the closeness the moment demands.

Mrs. Moreau watches Elise move through the steps and nods in approval.

"You are already perfect," she decides. "Leo, you need more practice with your footwork. Rotate with the others now."

Leo huffs in protest. "I can do it."

"Then prove it," Mrs. Moreau replies briskly. "Again, from the top. With a new partner."

And just like that, he is paired with the other girls.

Elise watches from the side of the stage as Leo twirls Marie Parker, his hands steady at her waist. Then Sophie Harris, who stumbles, laughing, as he catches her effortlessly.

She tells herself it is just blocking, just another part of the play.

And yet—something hot and unfamiliar coils in her chest.

He did not look at me like that when we danced.

Her fingers tighten around her script. She forces herself to look away, but it is too late. The feeling has already settled, heavy and unwanted.

She should not care. It is just a rehearsal. It does not matter.

And yet—

The next time Leo's eyes flick toward her, she is gone.

She does not know why she runs.

She only knows that suddenly, she is outside in the town square, hidden in the shadows of the clock tower, tears slipping down her cheeks.

She hates this.

Hates that after all this time, after all the silence and the distance, he still has the power to make her feel like this.

A familiar voice cuts through the quiet.

"Marlowe."

She freezes. Then, slowly, she wipes her eyes and turns.

Leo stands there, hands in his pockets, watching her with that look. The one she knows too well—the one that sees through every wall she tries to build.

"You left," he says simply.

Elise lifts her chin. "So?"

"So..." He exhales, stepping closer. "Were you jealous?"

She glares at him. "Do not flatter yourself."

A slow, knowing grin spreads across his face. "You were."

Elise looks away, jaw tight.

Leo leans against the stone wall beside her, quiet for a moment. Then, softly—

"You will always be my Beatrice, you know."

Something in her chest tightens.

Leo tilts his head, studying her. Then, with a teasing glint in his eyes, he adds, "But more importantly—what about our future kids? The world would not be ready for them, don't you think?"

Elise blinks. "What?"

"Our kids," he repeats, completely serious. "They would have my musical genius and your artistic brilliance. Imagine it—your fire, my flair. Dangerous combination. The world would not stand a chance."

For a long moment, she just stares at him.

Then—despite herself, despite everything—

She laughs.

A real, unburdened laugh.

And just like that, for the first time in a long, long while—

They are Leo and Elise again.

But only just.

Later, alone in her room, Elise sits by the window, knees pulled to her chest, chin resting atop them. Below, the streets glisten faintly with mist, the air tinged with the scent of smoke and mulched leaves.

She replays the evening like a scene, trying to tuck it neatly into her memory. But it won't stay still.

You will always be my Beatrice.

Sweet, maddening boy.

He says it like a promise. But Shakespeare was a playwright, not a prophet. And emotions, Elise knows, do not always follow the script.

She exhales, fingers tracing idle patterns on the windowpane.

He writes, does not he? Observes. Stores things.
What if I am just a story to him, someday? A study in contradictions.
What if one day, I am his subject?
Captured in lines I never gave him permission to write.

She shuts her eyes, but the thought lingers—an ache beneath her laughter, a stone beneath her pillow.

Across Wesley Lane, Leo lies awake too.

The stars outside are faint. The kind of night that folds quietly in on itself.

He thinks of her smirk. Her eyes when they are angry. The way her voice cracked around his name before she laughed again.

He meant what he said. He always does when it comes to her. But Elise—Elise is no fixed thing. She burns too bright to be held still.

And after everything—
What if she leaves me again?
What if next time, I cannot follow?

He turns onto his side and closes his eyes.
Neither of them speaks their doubts aloud.
But they carry them all the same.
   Like footnotes scribbled in the margins.
Like secrets tucked in stage directions...

IV

Among Scripts and Shadows

By the time they reach the end of Year 9, Leo and Elise are inseparable once more.

Not in the way they were as children-no, something has shifted.

They believe they have learned how not to wound each other.

How to leave space where, before, they might have rushed in.

They still tease, still spark and bicker, still laugh like no one else exists. But now, it is laced with care. With wariness, somewhat.

They have grown into their silences.

And they have learned that no matter how far they drift, something always—always—pulls them back.

Now, they cling to each other fiercely, as though trying to press time into pause.

There is no label, no definition—only a tether between

them that neither questions too closely.

And the drama room binds them.

It always has. It always will.

They take on the school plays together—Leo weaving magic into the scripts, adapting scenes with wit and longing, his dialogue always skimming too close to confession. Elise directs, commanding the chaos into shape, moulding their classmates into something almost transcendent.

Their plays are talked about for weeks after. Not because of grandeur or spectacle, but because they feel alive. Like every scene carries some secret meant only for the two of them.

More often than not, they land the leading roles. Not because of favouritism—though whispers always follow—but because no one else sets the stage alight like they do.

"Convenient, is it not?" Leo smirks one evening as they rehearse in the empty auditorium.

Elise, teetering on a rickety chair to adjust the stage lights, glances down at him. "Convenient, or well-earned?"

He tilts his head. "A bit of both, I think."

The smile they share is not smug. It is layered with history, near-losses, and the ache of things not said.

They both know the truth.

No one else could be Roxane to his Cyrano. Juliet to his Romeo. Marguerite to his Faust.

No one else could stand beside him like this—and that, perhaps, is the scariest part.

But together, they get away with everything.

They slip out of class more often than they should, always with a perfectly timed excuse.

"Mrs. Havers asked us to check the costumes in storage,"

Elise will say.

"Lighting tests for tomorrow," Leo will add, not missing a beat.

Their teachers sigh but let them go.

Mrs. Moreau turns a blind eye, always with a faint smile, as if she, too, remembers a time when youth felt like this.

Sometimes, they sneak off to Calloway's Bookshop. Elise balances on the ladder, flipping through poetry anthologies, while Leo leans against the shelves, idly tapping invisible piano keys.

"This one," Elise says one afternoon, holding up a weathered copy of Rilke.

"Too depressing," Leo decides.

"That is the point," she replies. "If we do not suffer, how will we ever be great?"

He snorts. "You are insufferable when you're in your tortured artist mood."

Other days, they cycle through the winding streets of Riversley. Elise swerves through narrow alleys, fearless, her laughter bright and reckless. Leo, ever dramatic, takes the bumpiest paths, his handlebars rattling dangerously.

"You are terrible at this," Elise laughs, watching him pluck crushed daisies from his hair.

"I would rather crash with flair than ride in a straight line," he grins.

In the quiet between golden hours, they climb onto the rooftop of St. Mary's Church. There, they lie side by side, watching the sky fade from blue to violet, sharing half-truths and hidden hopes.

"Do you think we will still be like this in ten years?" Elise asks one evening.

Leo, arms folded behind his head, replies, "Of course. Who else would tolerate me?"

She rolls her eyes, but her smile lingers.

Still, a breath later, she turns her face away.

She does not ask the real question: *What if we are not?*

He does not say what sits heavy in his chest: *What if you leave again?*

Because beneath the closeness, there is a new distance too. A soft wariness that neither speaks of. The kind that grows in the cracks of things once broken.

They are best friends again—almost.

But not quite.

Not like before, when everything was simple.

Now, they carry certain unspoken things.

They share secrets and laughter, but there is a line neither of them crosses.

Maybe it is safety.

Maybe it is fear.

Because somewhere between the scripts and stolen afternoons, their feelings have grown roots, deep and tangled. But naming them might ruin everything.

So instead, they pretend.

They speak in metaphors. In borrowed lines.

They wrap their truths in costumes and curtains, in piano notes and spotlight shadows.

And for now, that's enough.

There are still Calloway's and caramel sweets.

There are still rooftops and rehearsals.

And always, always,

The sound of a piano playing in the distance—a melody unfinished.

V
Chasing Different Stars

Elise and Leo walk into their final year at Riversley High as effortlessly as breathing. It is the year of GCSEs, of restless study sessions, of teachers drilling past paper questions into their heads, of highlighters staining their fingertips.

They take the same subjects—English Literature, History, Drama, and Art—a mix of their shared passions, where they can always count on each other. In English, they pass notes hidden inside poetry books. In History, they make up absurd stories to remember dates. In Art, they steal each other's brushes when the other is not looking. And in Drama—well, in Drama, they own the stage.

Their worlds shrink to just this: stolen moments in the library, Leo tapping his pencil against his notebook while Elise sketches absentmindedly on the back of his hand. Whispered frustrations about coursework, dramatic reenactments of Shakespeare in the common room, endless cups of cheap vending machine tea.

They study together, quizzing each other under the dim glow of streetlights on the walk home. Elise is the disciplined one, the one who colour-codes her notes and schedules revision sessions. Leo is the chaotic one, who swears by last-minute cramming and "studying through osmosis" by sleeping on his textbooks.

Yet, when Results Day arrives, they both do brilliantly. They open their envelopes with bated breath, hearts trembling beneath school blazers. And when they see their grades, relief washes over them like a tide—swift, overwhelming, and oddly bittersweet.

There is cheering in the halls, arms flung around necks, tear-stained cheeks pressed together. But beneath it all is a quiet grief no one names—the slow realisation that a chapter is closing.

Summer that year feels different. Softer, almost sacred.

Leo and Elise spend long hours at Calloway's, under trees, on park benches—nowhere in particular, but always close. They speak of futures like they are stories they have only half-written. They laugh about city universities and coffee addictions, about essays they will hate and people they have not met yet. But something unspoken trembles underneath: the ache of growing up, the terror of growing apart.

And just like that, September arrives.

They step into St. Aldwyn's Sixth Form College.

The campus is larger, the corridors unfamiliar, the faces mostly new. The school ties are gone, replaced with casual clothes that suddenly seem to define social status. The groups are different, the dynamics unspoken but deeply understood—people who travel in clusters, who already seem to know how to belong.

For the first time in years, Leo and Elise are not just "Leo and Elise" anymore.

They take their A-Levels—English Literature and Drama together, but Elise chooses History and Art, while Leo picks Music and Film Studies. At first, it does not feel like a loss. They still share two subjects. They still grab lunch together. They still text each other during boring lessons.

But little things shift.

Leo flourishes in St. Aldwyn's in a way that surprises even him. His natural charm, the way he walks like he owns the space without trying, his ability to make people laugh—it all draws attention. He becomes a presence at parties, someone people gravitate toward, someone who always has a joke, a smirk, a perfectly timed line.

And the attention changes him, even if he does not realise it.

Where once he and Elise spent free periods on their own, now he is surrounded by people. Where once he used to walk home with her, now he has plans—gatherings, parties, a group project that suddenly turns into a late-night hangout.

He flirts more now—casually, effortlessly. A raised eyebrow, a teasing comment, a hand brushing against an arm. It does not mean anything, not really. It is just fun. But fun has a way of looking real to the people who do not know him like Elise does.

Elise sees it all.

She sees the girls watching him, the way they linger, the way they laugh too loudly at his jokes. She tells herself it doesn't matter. She is busy, after all.

Because she, too, after all, is ELISE.

She has always been confident, but now people notice her in a way they never did before. Maybe it is the way she speaks in class—sharp, unwavering, the kind of intelligence that makes people listen. Maybe it is the way her art is now displayed in the halls, teachers murmuring about talent and future exhibitions. Maybe it is just that she no longer blends into the background.

And attention—true, meaningful attention—can be intoxicating.

There are new faces. People who ask her opinion and listen like it matters. People who invite her to join study groups, coffee outings, and weekend trips to the city.

And so, without meaning to, they begin to drift.

It is not dramatic. Not a fight. Not a betrayal. Just a slow and quiet drift—a space that neither of them notices until it has already taken root. Perhaps it is a distance they create without meaning to, a silent response to the fear of what might happen if they stay too close, if they begin to expect too much, and then end up disappointed.

They know each other well, perhaps too well in some ways. But not completely. There are still corners of their minds left untouched, thoughts unspoken, questions left unasked. And maybe that is the problem—they do not fully trust themselves with what those answers might be.

Like many teenagers, they are drawn more to what sparkles than to what is steady. Dreams feel louder than truth. What they want often eclipses what they already have. Leo chases the rush of admiration, the feeling of being seen in every room he walks into. Elise begins to crave the kind of attention that makes her feel like more than just the girl with paint-stained fingers.

They convince themselves it does not matter. That no distance could ever truly undo what they share. That they will always find their way back to one another. For now, Elise and Leo can wait, they believe.

But dreams are fragile. And space—once created—is not always easy to close.

VI

Unwritten Tomorrows

The final year at St. Aldwyn's arrives with a weight neither of them can ignore.

It is a year of last things—last autumn mornings in the library, last hurried coffees before class, last lingering conversations in the quiet corners of the campus.

And yet, it is also a year of firsts—first university applications, first real glimpses of the futures they have shaped for themselves, first moments of understanding that soon, everything will change.

They still move in parallel, but their paths have begun to drift, almost imperceptibly.

Leo's notebooks are filled with screenplays now—half-finished ideas, scribbled dialogues, scenes that only exist in his mind until he breathes them into being. His essays in English Literature have taken a dramatic turn, less analysis and more narrative, as though he is trying to write his way out of the present.

"Have you thought about film school?" Mr. Andrews asks one day, flipping through his coursework. Leo only grins, a little shyly, but the thought takes root. By winter, he is finalizing his application to study Film and Screenwriting at a university in Everstead. The idea of the city thrills him—the pulse of it, the noise, the anonymity. The space to become someone he is not yet sure how to be.

Elise, on the other hand, is still drawn to lines and light, to the way space breathes and buildings hold stories. Her sketchbooks are dense with cities that do not yet exist—bridges that twist like ribbons, glass towers that catch entire sunsets. Her Art and Design tutor suggests architecture, and the word settles into her like fate. She applies to Calderwich, known for its visionary programs and brutalist beauty.

She does not tell Leo how she chose it. And he does not ask.

They speak, of course. They still laugh. But now there are pauses.
Misunderstandings. Silences. Formal greetings.
A missed call that Leo does not return quickly enough.
A message Elise reads and chooses not to reply to right away.
He forgets her portfolio review date—just once—but the hurt stays.
She does not show up for his short film screening, citing coursework, though they both know she could have made it.
He praises someone else's artwork in front of her, and something in her chest twists.
She critiques one of his scripts—too harshly, maybe—and he goes quiet, for hours.
None of it is dramatic. There are no slammed doors, no name-calling.

Just a thousand tiny fractures. And in the spaces between, pride digs in.

Elise cannot explain the sharpness that sometimes enters her voice when he hesitates to share something real. She hates that she notices when he flinches—just slightly—at her tone.

He has always loved her fire. But sometimes, lately, he seems afraid of getting burned.

He begins to censor himself.

She begins to test him. He never fights back. And that only makes her angrier.

And what once felt like easy rhythm now feels like walking a wire in the wind.

Both Everstead and Calderwich are far from Riversley—and in their own way, far from each other.

The distance is no longer imagined. It is on paper. In confirmed offers. In the train maps and term dates.

The UCAS applications go through, each form a silent confirmation of the diverging lines they are drawing. They do not talk about it. Not really.

But it hangs in the air between them—this unspoken knowing.

They are still Leo and Elise.

But now, there are spaces between them.

Wounds too small to name, but too deep to ignore.

And so the year rushes forward. Exams loom. Futures crystallize.

They try to hold on. Or pretend to.

And before it all ends, before the corridors of St. Aldwyn's become just another chapter in their shared past, there is one final tradition—

The farewell ball.

VII

Ink and Ashes

The hall gleams under strings of fairy lights, the grand chandelier casting golden reflections onto the polished floor. St. Aldwyn's has spared no effort—this is their night, the end of an era, a moment suspended between youth and the unknown.

Elise arrives on the arm of Daniel Hale, the boy she has recently begun dating and believes she loves. He is steady, kind, and predictable in a way that soothes her. They plan to study architecture together at Calderwich, already mapping out their future. Tonight, he holds her hand as if she is his whole world, and she allows herself to believe that maybe, just maybe, this is the beginning of something lasting.

Then Leo walks in.

He is dressed sharply—his tux perfectly tailored, his hair effortlessly tousled—but it is not his appearance that turns heads. It is the girl beside him. She is breathtaking in a deep crimson gown, her presence commanding attention. She is exactly the kind of girl Leo would bring—someone to make a statement, someone to flaunt.

Elise should not care.

Yet, when Leo's gaze sweeps the crowd and lands on her, lingering for just a second too long, something in her stomach twists.

The evening unfolds with a blur of traditions. Speeches are given, memories shared. Teachers raise a toast to futures unknown. Then, as the night deepens, the music shifts, and the first dance begins. The honoured tradition of the leavers' waltz—a moment for partners to move together one last time before stepping into the world.

Elise dances with Daniel. Leo, with his date. But there are moments, fleeting and sharp, where their eyes meet across the ballroom.

A change of partners. Another tradition.

And suddenly, Elise is in Leo's arms.

The air crackles between them. His hand is warm at the small of her back; her fingers tremble in his. The music swells around them, but neither speaks.

Leo looks at her—really looks at her. She is stunning tonight, her hair swept into a loose knot, a few strands framing her face, and the deep red dress clinging to her like flame, catching the light with every step she takes. But it is more than that. She has always been stunning to him, even when she was covered in charcoal smudges and biting at his wit. But tonight, something is different. Maybe it is the fact that soon, they will part ways, that in mere months, she will be gone. Maybe it is the way her lashes lower when his gaze lingers too long.

"Having fun?" he finally murmurs.

Elise does not trust her voice, so she nods.

He spins her, pulling her back smoothly, his grip firm. "Daniel is lucky," he adds, almost too casually.

And just like that, the moment shatters. Elise stiffens, stepping back the second the dance ends.

"Come with me," Leo says suddenly.

She hesitates. Then, before she can think better of it, she follows him out into the corridor.

Leo reaches into his pocket and pulls out an envelope. His fingers brush over it almost hesitantly before he holds it out to her.

"What is this?" Elise frowns.

"Just read it," he says.

Her fingers tremble as she unfolds the paper. His handwriting, looping and familiar, fills the page.

"Elise,

You will leave soon, and I do not know how to say this out loud. But I have been having dreams. Dreams of you in white, standing beneath a sky so wide it steals my breath. Dreams where I look at you, and nothing else in the world matters. Not music, not cinema—just you.

And I think—I know—that you have always been the answer to the questions I never knew how to ask.

So, before we step into different lives, I need you to know: I have realised. You are the one, always have been. Without knowing, I have always loved you in every version of myself, even the ones too foolish to understand it—"

Elise stops reading.

Because suddenly, she is thirteen again, sitting in the library, editing the very same words in his letters to other girls.

Fury floods her veins.

"Unbelievable," she breathes.

Leo frowns. "Elise?"

She shoves the letter back into his hands. "Is this a joke?"

Confusion flashes across his face. "What?"

"You think you can just—" She swallows, the lump in her throat threatening to choke her. "You think I am like them? Just another name on your list? Like that stupid wannabe model you walked in with?"

Realization dawns in his eyes, and something in his face hardens.

"Elise—"

"No." She shakes her head. "I thought—" Her voice cracks. She does not finish.

She crumples the letter in her fist and shoves it against his chest.

Leo stares at her, and something inside him shatters.

He had been a fool.

A fool to think she would see. A fool to believe she would know that this was different.

That she was different.

Anger coils in his chest, sharp and burning. His ego, his pride—every defense he has ever built—takes over.

Fine.

If she wants to believe he is that person, he will be.

Without another word, he turns on his heel, walks back into the ballroom, and—before he can stop himself—grabs his date and kisses her.

A murmur spreads through the crowd. Some whistle, some laugh. His date giggles against his lips.

Elise watches from the corridor, her breath shallow.

For a second, just a second, she thinks of her own dreams. The ones she has never spoken of. The ones where she walks through sunlit halls, turns a corner, and finds him waiting for her.

But maybe she had been wrong.

Maybe this is how it was always meant to be.

She feels a tear slip down her cheek.

Daniel finds her moments later, asking if she wants to leave.

She nods.

And just like that, the night—their last night together—ends.

VIII

Echoes of the Unsaid

Leo steps into Everstead University with the boundless thrill of reinvention. Here, no one knows him as Elise's best friend, as the boy who played piano at every school event. In Everstead, he is just Leo. A blank slate. A rising star. The world is his to shape.

He thrives in the pulse of it—late-night script readings, heated debates over film theory, the first taste of true creative freedom. His screenwriting professor calls his first short script "startlingly raw." The way Leo writes dialogue, the rhythm of his pacing—there is something alive in his work that makes people pay attention. By winter, he writes and directs a short film that sweeps a university-wide competition, and his name starts passing through the right circles.

And then, there is the social scene.

If Riversley had made him charming, Everstead turns him magnetic. He plays the piano at student bars, drawing admiration with every effortless note. Women are drawn to him, and for this time, he allows himself to indulge further. He dates freely, enjoys the attention, never stays too long. No messy endings. No attachments. No regrets. He does not look back at Riversley.

The second year pushes him even higher. His professors notice him. They introduce him to industry professionals, and suddenly, his name begins to mean something outside of Everstead's walls. Over the summer, he lands an internship at an independent film studio in Alderidge—a city buzzing with artistic energy, a hub for film and theatre.

He begins watching real directors work, studying the way stories are shaped on screen. One of his screenplays makes it into the hands of an industry contact. Later that year, he is invited to a student film festival, where his work is shortlisted. The momentum is unstoppable.

And with success comes reputation.

Leo becomes known for his quick wit and quiet eccentricity, the way he always knows exactly what to say. There is an allure in his confidence, the way he moves through the world as if he owns it. Women notice, and are desperate to get close. But Leo, although charming, is detached, always slightly out of reach. Relationships never last—he loses interest too easily, too quickly. He tells himself it is better this way. Elise never calls. Neither does he. Maybe it is for the best.

By his third year, he is exactly where he wants to be. His final-year project—a screenplay set to be showcased in front of industry professionals—is his ticket to the life he has spent years chasing. The future he has dreamt of is finally within reach.

And then, one day, the phone rings.

At first, he barely registers the unknown number. He almost ignores it. But something makes him pick up.

"Is this Leo? This is Isla's mother."

For a moment, the name does not mean anything. And then, it does.

Isla Davenport.

He has not thought about her in years. The girl he had taken to the farewell ball. His gorgeous date—tall, elegant, always flawless. Too flawless.

She had been intense, always lingering too long, always making everything feel urgent. She had texted too much, called too often. She had wanted too much of him.

And he had ignored her.

After leaving Riversley, he had entertained her attention for a while, indulging the way she clung to him. But then the messages piled up, unread. She had called, and he had let the phone ring. Eventually, she had stopped. And that was that.

Or so he thought.

Now, her mother's voice is unsteady, every word a thread unraveling.

"She is not well, Leo. She quit modeling. She is back home. She has been asking for you."

He exhales, rubbing a hand over his face. He has deadlines. A screening in two days. He cannot afford distractions. His graduation date is quite near.

"She only wants to see you once."

There is something fragile in the way her mother says it, but Leo shakes his head. Isla had always overreacted, turned small things into catastrophes. She would be fine.

But the next day, he hears the final straw.

Isla had attempted to end her life the very night of the day he had spoken with her mother.

The news lands like a punch to the gut. Not loud. Just... absolute.

The city lights, once dazzling, now seem sterile. His successes, awards, praise, and polished scripts feel like hollow applause in an empty theatre.

And for the first time in three years, Leo packs his bags without hesitation. No calculated pause. No justifications.

He boards the train to Riversley before he can talk himself out of it.

As the countryside blurs past, the ache in his chest sharpens into something clearer. Not guilt, exactly. Something older.

A slow-burning shame.

Had he been running all this time, not from pain, but from responsibility?

He had always believed he left people gently. That his silences were soft enough not to scar. That he did not allow them to come too close or bond too much. Everyone healed, eventually, just as he had.

But Isla had not.

And maybe, God, he hoped, maybe she was not the only one who had held on.

IX

The Reckoning of Hearts

The moment Leo steps off the train, a strange hollowness grips him. Riversley looks the same—too familiar, too unchanged—but something in him is not. He used to think coming home would always feel effortless, like slipping back into an old song. But now, the station feels too quiet, the air too heavy, as if the town itself knows he is not the same boy who left. The thrill of returning is missing. In its place, a quiet unease lingers.

He drives past the high street, past Wren & Quill where he and Elise used to steal moments between school and home. He does not stop. He keeps going, past his old school, past Calloway's, which still stands—the sign crooked and the window displays a tad quieter.

But for a moment, he sees his younger self in the glass—careless, certain, unaware of how years would hollow him out in places he never thought could break. Yes, everything is familiar, but they seem not to welcome him.

His mother is relieved to see him but does not ask too many questions. She senses it—this is not just a visit. Something heavier has brought him back. He does not unpack. He barely sits before heading out again, making his way to the address Isla's mother had given him.

She lives on the quieter side of town now, far from the lights of Veridien's Lane, where she once belonged. The house is modest, small, nothing like the sleek apartment she used to post pictures from. When the door opens, it is not Isla who stands there but her mother, a tired woman with worry lining her face.

"She is in her room," she says simply. "Go on up."

He steps inside. The house smells of lavender and something faintly medicinal, like too many sleepless nights spent waiting. The air is heavy, as if sorrow has settled into the walls. He takes the stairs slowly, his fingers grazing the wooden banister. His heart beats against his ribs, loud and uncertain.

When he pushes open her door, he hardly recognises her.

Isla sits by the window, knees drawn up, her silhouette thin against the grey light. Her once-glossy hair falls limply past her shoulders, her skin is paler than he remembers, and her eyes—God, her eyes. The light in them is gone.

She turns, slowly, as if moving through water. When she sees him, something flickers across her face. Surprise. Hope. Maybe something else.

"You came," she whispers.

He exhales, stepping inside, feeling like an intruder in the ruins of something he never truly understood. "Yeah," he says, voice rough. "I came."

Silence stretches between them, thick with all the things neither of them knows how to say.

Isla looks away first. "Mum begged you, did not she?"

"No." His voice is quiet. "I had to come."

She lets out a breath that isn't quite a laugh. "You had to?" Her lips curve, bitter. "That is a first."

Leo flinches. He deserves that.

She studies him for a moment before shaking her head. "I was so stupid," she murmurs, voice distant. "I thought I meant something to you. I thought that night—" She stops, swallowing. "You made me feel like I was the most beautiful girl in the room."

"You were," he says before he can stop himself.

Her gaze snaps to his, sharp with something that almost looks like anger. "That was the problem, was not it?" Her voice is barely above a whisper. "You wanted beauty. Not me."

He does not answer. He does not need to. The truth is there, between them, a wound long left to fester.

She looks away, biting her lip. "I thought... if I just held on a little longer, you would see me."

Leo swallows the lump in his throat. His hands clench at his sides. "Isla, I never meant to hurt you."

"But you did." The words are quiet, resigned. "And the worst part is... you did not even notice."

He exhales sharply, running a hand through his hair. "I do not know how to love, Isla. I do not think I ever did."

Her eyes search his face, looking for something—he does not know what. Forgiveness? Understanding? Closure?

He shakes his head, looking away. "I thought... I thought winning over beauty meant something. That it was power. Pride." He laughs, but it is hollow. "I never thought about what happened after."

"That is because you never stayed long enough to care."

The truth of it crushes him.

For the first time, he sees himself through her eyes. A boy who moved too fast, who loved the chase but never the stillness that followed. Who collected glances and whispers like trophies, only to discard them when the shine faded. He had been reckless with people's hearts, not because he wanted to hurt them, but because he never thought he could.

Isla looks back out of the window. "I do not need you to love me, Leo," she says softly. "I just needed to know I was not nothing to you."

Leo closes his eyes for a moment, his chest tight with something raw, something painfully new. He steps forward, reaching for her hand. She does not pull away.

"You were not nothing," he says. "I see that now. And I am sorry. For everything."

She nods, just once. It is not forgiveness, not yet. But maybe, someday.

As he leaves, the weight of his past lingers behind him, but another settles in its place.

He thinks of all the faces—the ones that had looked at him with admiration, adoration, even love. How easily he had taken them for granted, as if their feelings were his to play with. As if his own wounds, his own insecurities, justified the hurt he caused.

No more.

Whatever he has lost, whatever he is still searching for, it is no one else's burden to bear.

Pride, solitude, fear—these are his own battles.

He will not use another person's heart as a shield. He will not break someone just to feel whole.

For the first time in his life, Leo realises—if he wants to be better, he has to start by facing himself.

X

Blueprints of Doubt

On the other hand, Elise's world expands the moment she steps into Calderwich University. The sprawling campus, the neoclassical buildings with their grand facades, the scent of old books and fresh ink—it is everything she had dreamed of. The architecture department is housed in a sleek, glass-fronted building that feels like a promise of the future, and the moment she steps inside, she knows she belongs here.

Her first year is exhilarating. She is surrounded by students just as passionate as she is, people who speak in the language of design, who dream of shaping cities, of drawing not just buildings but entire worlds. She soaks it all in—the late-night studio sessions, the debates about function versus form, the rush of presenting a project and watching a professor nod in approval.

Academically, she shines. Her ability to blend artistry with precision makes her stand out. One of her early projects—a reimagination of a Gothic cathedral with modern sustainability elements—earns her a glowing review from her tutor.

"You have an instinct for this, Elise," Professor Howard tells her after one of her presentations. "It is rare to see someone with such a natural grasp of both structure and aesthetics."

The praise fuels her. She throws herself deeper into her work, sketching endlessly, poring over design journals, spending hours in the drafting studio. She hardly notices how quickly the year passes.

And through it all, there is Daniel.

Daniel, who had been by her side since Riversley, who shares her love for architecture, who is reliable, steady, and always there. They had come to university together, and everything feels as though it is unfolding exactly as it should. They work late into the nights side by side, swapping ideas, building each other up. They walk through the streets of Calderwich, admiring the old stone bridges, the towering spires, and dreaming of the buildings they will one day create.

It is easy, comforting. She is happy.

Or at least, she thinks she is.

Because, by her second year, Elise is at the top of her class. Her professors take note of her precision, her ability to balance creativity with technical skill. She is given more responsibilities, asked to mentor first-years, and even recommended for a coveted internship at a prestigious architecture firm.

It is everything she has worked for. Everything she has wanted.

And yet, a small restlessness creeps in.

It is not in her work—there, she thrives. It is not in her friendships—she has built a close-knit circle of fellow students who challenge and inspire her. It is in Daniel.

Daniel, who is still wonderful. Who still looks at her the way he always has. Who still walks her home after late nights in the studio, who still holds her hand in the quiet corners of campus.

But something has changed.

Or maybe it is her.

She notices the way her laughter feels forced sometimes, the way their conversations feel repetitive. He still talks about their future—how they will graduate together, work at the same firm, build a life together. And for the first time, the thought does not bring her comfort. It brings something closer to unease.

She tells herself it is just stress. That she is overthinking. That love is meant to feel like this—stable, predictable, safe.

But then, there is Oliver.

Oliver is in her third-year design module. He is effortlessly charismatic, with a sharp mind and a dry wit that keeps everyone on their toes. He challenges her in a way Daniel never has—picking apart her ideas, forcing her to defend her designs, pushing her to think beyond the boundaries she has set for herself.

And she enjoys it.

At first, it is just intellectual sparring—heated debates over blueprints and models, long discussions about urban landscapes and the future of sustainable architecture. But then, it spills over into late-night coffees, shared glances across the studio, lingering conversations that stretch into the early hours.

She tells herself it is nothing. That she loves Daniel. That Oliver is just a friend, a colleague, someone who excites her creatively, nothing more.

But then there are the moments when Daniel kisses her, and her mind wanders. When she catches herself looking for Oliver in a crowded lecture hall. When her pulse quickens—not at the sight of her boyfriend, but at the thought of someone else.

It terrifies her.

She has always been a firm believer in loyalty, in true love, and in fairytale endings. She has never been the kind of person to waver, to stray. And yet, here she is, standing at the edge of something she cannot name.

By the time her final year begins, she can no longer deny it—her heart is not where it should be.

She tries to fight it. She buries herself in work, convinces herself that this is just a phase, that Daniel is still the man she is meant to be with. She holds on tighter, tells herself she just needs to try harder.

But love is not something that can be forced.

One evening, as they walk through the city, Daniel reaches for her hand, and for the first time, she hesitates. It is small, almost imperceptible, but he notices.

"Elise," he says softly. "What is wrong?"

She opens her mouth, but no words come. Because she does not know.

She should love him. She should feel the same certainty he does.

But she does not.

And the worst part? She has no reason. Daniel has done nothing wrong. There is no betrayal, no great conflict, no tragic misunderstanding.

Only the quiet, aching truth that sometimes, love fades—not with a storm, but with a whisper.

And Elise finds herself lost in a way she never thought she would be.

XI

When the Past Comes Calling

Two days before her graduation, Elise is seated in the university studio, hunched over her desk, surrounded by blueprints, sketches, and scale models. The final project of her undergraduate degree looms over her like a towering structure, demanding perfection. Her fingers, streaked with graphite and ink, move with obsessive precision. The world outside does not exist—not the laughter from the hallway, not the faint breeze curling in through the half-open window.

And then her phone rings.

She barely looks at it at first—just another reminder, probably, about the submission deadline.

But something pulls her gaze.

A number she does not recognise.

Still, a twist tightens in her stomach. Instinct, maybe. Memory.

She answers.

"Hello?"

The voice that comes through is jagged, sharp, unmistakably familiar—yet wrong somehow. Older. Angrier.

"So this is what you do now?"

She goes still.

"You disappear for three bloody years," Leo says, "And then act like I am the ghost?"

Elise blinks, heart picking up pace. "Leo?"

He does not acknowledge the name. Only keeps going, voice gathering venom.

"You know, I waited," he spits. "Thought maybe you would reach out. Just a line. A text. A damn question—'Are you still breathing?' But no. Not even that."

"You left," she snaps, standing now, as if the walls are closing in. "You vanished first, Leo. You do not get to turn this around."

He lets out a hollow laugh. "You always were good at flipping the story. Makes it easier, does not it? Pretending I am the one who disappeared."

"Oh, do not start," she mutters, trying to steady her voice. "You want to talk uncomfortable? Try being ghosted by your best friend without a word. Without a goodbye. That messes with your head."

"And you want to talk about betrayal?" he hisses. "You did not even try, Elise. You did not call. You did not write. You did not are."

"I did care!" she fires back. "But you made it very clear you did not. You walked away without looking back—into your shiny new world like Riversley was some stain you could not wait to scrub off."

"You think I had it easy?" His voice rises. "You think I walked away untouched?"

"Do not pretend you gave a damn," she snaps. "You were always surrounded by someone new. Someone laughing at your jokes, circling you like moths. Isla, Colette, the rest of them—"

"Do not," he cuts in, voice low and dangerous. "Do not you dare speak their names like you know what happened."

She falls silent.

His breath rasps through the phone. "Isla tried to end her life the same night I spoke to her mum. Did you know that?"

The words hit her square in the chest. Cold. Final.

"I spoke to her, knowing I was the one who pushed her there. Knowing it was my fault. Because I did not call. Because I never looked back. Because I thought people would move on as fast as I did. But she did not."

Her voice drops, trembling. "Leo... I did not know."

"No," he replies, dead cold. "You did not. Because you were not there."

"Do not shift the blame on me," she spits.

"You are still defending yourself Els. Don't you feel at least a bit sorry for her?"

Silence stretches. Heavy. Gritty.

Then, like a knife:

"Or were you too busy playing house with Daniel or whoever the hell it is now?"

"Do not," she warns, voice tight.

"Do not what?" he snaps. "Do not talk about your perfect life? Do not mention the fact that you replaced me without missing a step?"

Her pulse pounds. Her throat burns.

"I did not replace you."

"Oh, you did. And you know what?" His voice turns to steel. "Maybe you were right. Maybe I was never worth keeping around."

A breath.

"But I will tell you something, Elise—you sure as hell were not worth chasing either."

And then—

Click.

The line goes dead.

She stares at her phone, breath shallow, knuckles white around the edges.

Leo.

Leo, who had once been her gravity. Her softness. Her storm.

Now—

Sharp edges.

Venom.

She presses the phone to her forehead and draws a long, deliberate breath.

Then she moves out of the studio and into the kitchen.

The kettle hums behind her. She does not wait. The coffee burns her tongue, but she lets it. She needs the sting.

Two days.

In two days, she would graduate.

And Leo could stay wherever the hell he was—sinking in his anger, swallowed by his silence.

She would not follow.

Not this time.

XII

Unfinished Sentences

Leo pours himself another measure of scotch, watching as the amber liquid swirls in the glass before settling. The air in his Everstead flat feels heavy, thick with silence, as if the walls are closing in. The city outside hums with life, but inside, it is just him, the drink in his hand, and the thoughts clawing their way through his mind.

He had returned two days before graduation, expecting the familiar rush of anticipation, the satisfaction of having conquered three years in one of the best universities in the country. He had done it—he had thrived, excelled, and outshone expectations. He had played the part of the golden boy, the rising star, the one with talent and charm and a future already paved before him.

But none of it feels the way it should.

The laughter at the bars, the admiration in people's eyes, the clink of glasses raised to success—everything feels muted, distant.

Because the moment he stops moving, stops distracting himself, the question creeps in.

How do you correct yourself if you refuse to face your reflection? And was not that the promise he had made to himself when he left Riversley? To stop using people as crutches for his own insecurities, to stop burying his flaws beneath borrowed affections and fleeting distractions? Had he not vowed to take responsibility for the damage he had caused, to stop hurting others for his own escapes?

Then why does he still feel like a fraud? Why does the hollow space inside him feel as deep as ever?Why does it still burn—that memory of Isla, her fragile smile, her mother's quiet gratitude, as though Leo himself had pulled her daughter back from the brink?

Had he really helped her? Or had he just sought absolution? Had it been about her at all? Or just another attempt to silence the ache within himself? And if he is still running in circles, still incapable of being honest with himself—then how does he even begin to fix it? How do you become better if you refuse to examine the pieces of yourself that are broken?

And is not Elise the closest thing he has ever had to a mirror? Is not she the one who was supposed to be his reflection—the only person who had ever understood him without him uttering a word?

Leo grips the glass tighter, his jaw clenching.

She had seen him before anyone else had. Had known him beyond the words he spoke, had understood the silences between them. She had always been the one who saw past the masks, past the bravado.

But when it had mattered—when he had finally laid himself bare—she had refused to see.

Leo downs another drink, but it is nothing compared to the fire rising inside him.

He pulls open the drawer and takes out his journal, where he had stuffed it away—the letter he had given her, the one she had shoved back into his hands. The creases from where she had crushed it are still there, the paper slightly crumpled, as if bruised. He smooths it out, but the damage remains.

Just like him.

His own words stare back at him—words she had not even bothered to read to their end.

"Elise,

You will leave soon, and I do not know how to say this out loud. But I have been having dreams. Dreams of you in white, standing beneath a sky so wide it steals my breath. Dreams where I look at you, and nothing else in the world matters. Not music, not cinema—just you.

And I think—I know—that you have always been the answer to the questions I never knew how to ask.

So, before we step into different lives, I need you to know: I have realised. You are the one, always have been. Without knowing, I have always loved you in every version of myself, even the ones too foolish to understand it.

And if you ever wake up one day and wonder if someone, somewhere, remembers you exactly as you are, if someone has memorised the way your voice curls around certain words, or how your brows knit together when you are lost in thought, then know that I have.

I have carried you with me in ways I do not think I will ever be able to undo.

And I do not want to.

There is no grand confession here, no request, no expectation. I just need you to know that loving you has been the quietest, truest thing I have ever done.

And if I had to live this life a thousand times over, I would find you in every single one.

Leo."

His grip tightens around the paper.

He had meant every word.

And yet, to her, it had been just another trick.

Something inside him snaps.

Leo tosses the letter onto the desk, reaching for the bottle of scotch again, but his hands are shaking now. He does not want to think. He does not want to feel this bitterness curling inside him, this ache of being misunderstood in the one moment he had been honest.

He downs another drink, then another, until the anger is not just inside him—it is thrumming through his veins, demanding an outlet.

Before he can second-guess it, he grabs his phone.

He does not care that they have not spoken in years. Does not care that she has likely moved on, that she probably has Daniel or whoever in her life now.

She had thrown him away like he was nothing. Like his words had meant nothing.

He dials.

And when she picks up, he does not let her speak.

His words are sharp, venomous, spilling through the line before he can stop them. He is not calculating his tone, not choosing the perfect words. He is tearing into her, voice laced with something he does not want to name—pain, betrayal, the kind of hurt that festers when you are dismissed by the one person who should have known better.

And she—defensive, as she always had been. Then furious.

Good. Let her feel it too.

By the time he hangs up, his heart is hammering, his breath unsteady.

The room feels colder now, as if he has drained the warmth from it himself.

The letter lies on the desk, still open, still half-read by the one person it was meant for.

Leo stares at it for a long time before he looks away.

This is why he does not let himself care.

Because when he does, it only ends in ruin. And yet, he folds the letter and puts it away into his journal again before dozing off, exhausted, on the table.

XIII

A Thousand Tomorrows, A Single Step

Graduation day arrives beneath a sky that cannot decide between sunshine and rain. The air hums with excitement, with farewells and futures, with a kind of collective nostalgia for a time not yet past. Families gather in clusters, cameras flash, and the weight of the day settles over Everstead like a held breath.

Leo stands among his peers in his graduation robes, the black fabric pressing down on his shoulders, heavier than it should be. Applause echoes through the hall as names are called, degrees conferred, and hands shaken. He steps onto the stage when his name is announced, accepting the certificate that marks the official beginning of everything he has worked for.

His professors nod approvingly, his peers cheer. He smiles, effortless as always, but inside, something shifts.

For years, he has worn his charm like armour, wielded it like a weapon. He has been the golden boy, the one who could walk into any room and make it his. But today, standing beneath the weight of his own name being spoken into the world, he makes a quiet promise to himself:

Never again. Never again will he use his charisma to take what he does not truly want, to seek validation where none is needed, to collect admiration like trinkets just to prove a point.

Maybe it is the first step to being a good man.

After the ceremony, he moves through the sea of well-wishers, shaking hands, posing for photographs, nodding at words of pride and expectation. But beneath it all, he feels the distance between who he was and who he wants to be stretch wider.

And then, somewhere in another city, at another graduation, Elise is standing on a stage of her own.

At Calderwich, Elise's name is called, and she ascends the stage with steady steps. Her fingers close around the diploma, a symbol of years of precision, late nights bent over blueprints, the constant hum of creation in her mind.

The audience claps. Her tutors smile. In the front row, Oliver beams, already talking about their year out placements—about the architecture firm they both received offers from, about finding a flat, about a future drawn neatly in lines and angles.

She should be thrilled. She should be basking in this moment. Instead, something inside her feels like an unfinished sketch, a plan abandoned mid-draft.

Oliver kisses her cheek when she returns to her seat, and she smiles, but her heart is somewhere else.

Because it is happening again.

She had once thought Daniel was it—the love that would anchor her, that would shape the foundation of her life. She had been so sure. And yet, over time, the certainty had frayed. Daniel had become a habit, a memory of something she once longed for but no longer did.

And now Oliver. Steady, kind, reliable Oliver. She had believed, once again, that this was what love was supposed to feel like. That this time, she had found it. That she had chosen correctly.

But why, then, does the feeling slip through her fingers like sand?

Why, when she looks at the future she has built, does she feel like something is missing?

She has no answers. Only a quiet decision that settles deep inside her:

Once she moves, she will move on.

Oliver is not her forever.

And that should terrify her. But instead, it just leaves her confused.

The ceremony ends, and somewhere, amid the cheers and champagne and the flurry of photographs, both Leo and Elise step forward in their different worlds—outwardly composed, inwardly uncertain.

XIV
Architecture of Emptiness

The halls of Calderwich—and Oliver—fade into the past, somewhere in that blur of her year out. A year meant for work and clarity, though for Elise, it becomes a quiet unraveling. By the time her offer from Greymoor's School of Architecture arrives, she already knows she will not be returning.

She has long dreamed of this next chapter—of Greymoor's experimental studios, its practicing mentors, and the city's calm, open rhythm. But more than its prestige, what draws her is its promise: space to think, to rebuild, and maybe, to begin again.

She is twenty-three, her portfolio gleaming with high praise, and her tutors speak of her with admiration—"One of the most promising minds in sustainable design," one had said during her final review.

Her days are structured, layered like the blueprints she drafts. Studio work, late-night research, and site visits fill her calendar. She is awarded a partial scholarship for her work on urban regeneration, and her designs are often featured in the department's showcases. The praise comes, the offers follow—.internships at boutique firms in Northleigh and Eldenham, even a summer workshop in Vesterhaven.

But if her academic life is sculpted and certain, her emotional world is crumbling beneath the surface.

She meets Luca during a design critique, a fellow student with olive skin and a quick, generous laugh. He sketches with wild passion, always talking about designing cities that feel like poems. They fall into an easy rhythm—coffee after lectures, long walks discussing Le Corbusier and dreams of building in Azarien. Elise finds herself drawn to his restlessness and ambition, his hands always smudged with pencil dust. He kisses her outside the studio after a rainstorm. It is gentle, curious.

But three months in, she begins to feel it again. That slow, creeping itch. Conversations with Luca begin to feel rehearsed. His dramatic flair now seems juvenile, his restlessness more like avoidance. One evening, he shows her a tattoo he got on impulse—a sketch of a staircase she once designed—and instead of being moved, Elise feels a strange kind of suffocation. Two weeks later, she ends it.

She tells herself it is fine. That love, perhaps, is not meant to last in a life filled with transient projects and moving cities. But something inside her starts to ache with every breakup, as though she is shedding parts of herself she can never quite reclaim.

Then comes Rowan, a structural engineer she collaborates with on a live housing project. Older, more stable. He smells of cedarwood and always remembers her coffee order. With Rowan, things are quieter. Dinners after site meetings, shared train rides, and him offering her his scarf on colder days. He is kind, intelligent, and grounded. Her parents talk to him often. They love him.

But six months in, Elise finds herself lying awake beside him, staring at the ceiling of her new flat in Greymoor's Northern Quarter. Rowan's arm is draped over her, his breathing steady. And yet, she feels lonelier than she ever did. His kindness no longer stirs her. His steadiness feels like stagnation.

One morning, she skips a meeting just to sit alone in the cafe where they first met. She looks around and wonders if she has become addicted to the idea of love rather than the thing itself. Each relationship begins with wonder, with sincerity, with the hope that this time it will be different. But time and again, the magic withers.

It is not them, she begins to realise. It is her. There is a restlessness inside her that even the grandest skylines and sweetest words cannot soothe. By twenty-five, she is exhausted—not just by work, but by herself.

She finishes her postgraduate studies with distinction, lands a full-time position at a heritage restoration firm in Westvale, a historic riverside city known for its Georgian architecture and thriving conservation scene.

Elise moves into a quiet one-bedroom flat overlooking a park, a few hours south of Riversley. She decorates it with minimalism, her favourite Bauhaus prints on the walls, fresh eucalyptus in the vases. The world sees a successful young architect with a bright future.

But Elise, in the solitude of her evenings, stands by her window with a glass of wine, and wonders:

Is there something in her that is irrevocably unfinished?

And why, no matter how carefully she builds her life, does it still feel like something essential is missing?

XV

The Stillness
Between Frames

After graduating from Everstead, Leo moves to the quiet town of Halewick—a stone's throw from the coast, known for its old cinemas and fog-draped alleyways that look like they have held a thousand stories. It is not glamorous, but that is precisely why he chooses it. Rather than chaos, Halewick offers space. Space to create, and maybe, to heal.

He joins a small but respected independent production house, Glasshouse Films, tucked inside a converted warehouse that smells of coffee, paint, and old reels. They make documentaries, experimental shorts, and the occasional indie feature. Leo starts as a script editor, then slowly works his way into writing and eventually co-directing small segments.

He works tirelessly, often losing himself in the silence of cutting rooms and midnight shoots. For the first time, success feels earned and not merely performed. His first co-written short, *"Salt in the Wound,"* screens at a festival in Brighton-on-Lure, and though it does not win, it draws enough attention to get him a modest commission from the indie wing of a nationally recognised media house.

But amid the steady climb, something inside Leo remains unsettled.

His past promises echo in the quiet moments—especially the one he made to himself after Isla: never to hurt, never to lead on, never to use affection as escape or validation. So, when women approach him after screenings or interviews, drawn to the now quiet charisma he wields with restraint, he politely distances himself.

Until her.

Her name is Clara Norwood.

She is a costume designer, newly hired on a feature film Glasshouse is consulting for. Not loud or overly charming, Clara has a kind of thoughtful beauty that does not ask to be seen. She notices the smallest things: how Leo scratches behind his ear when thinking, how he speaks to actors like he is writing as he goes. She never interrupts. She listens. And in that listening, she opens something Leo thought he had locked away for good.

Clara does not remind him of Elise. No. She reminds him of the absence Elise left—the mirror he lost, the reflection that once called him to account. But this is different. Clara's world is not tangled with memory. It is rooted in the present. Grounded. Safe.

Still, the feeling that creeps up inside him is not safety—it is fear. The kind that rises slowly and unannounced. The kind that settles in the chest like fog.

It begins innocently enough—proximity. Clara works in the same building, in the design wing that always smells faintly of fabric dyes and wood polish. She walks past Leo's edit suite nearly every morning with a thermos of tea tucked under one arm and a leather sketchbook in her hand. She nods politely, sometimes offers a wry smile. For a while, that is all.

Their first real conversation is not in the studio at all—it is in a dimly lit pub in Halewick, where the crew is half-heartedly celebrating the wrap of a particularly chaotic indie shoot. Clara sits alone at a corner table with a drink and a half-finished crossword. Leo, restless and tired of smiling, slides into the seat across from her and says, "You are the only one here not pretending to have a great time."

She quirks an eyebrow. "That is rich coming from you. You have looked bored since you walked in."

He laughs—genuinely. The kind of laugh that feels like an exhale. She points to the crossword. "Six-letter word for illusory comfort?"

"Hollow," he answers without hesitation.

Their eyes meet. Something shifts. Not dramatically. Just enough to change everything.

What follows is slow. Unfolding like a well-written scene—natural, unhurried. An exchange of playlists. A shared coffee in the green room. An impromptu walk home after a long day on set. Clara, with her careful restraint and observant gaze, does not rush anything. Leo, still rebuilding the scaffolding of his emotional world, finds comfort in her pace.

She never asks for more than he can give. She never expects him to explain the weight behind his silences. And that is what surprises him. The ease of it. The steadiness. There are no theatrics. No sweeping declarations. Just gestures—her fingertips brushing his when handing over a script, the way she folds napkins into tiny boats when thinking, how she once rested her head on his shoulder in a cab without saying a word.

One rainy evening in Halewick, after they have both slogged through back-to-back shoots, Clara invites him over. They make pasta, drink too much wine, and watch an old French film on mute while making up their own ridiculous dialogue. It is silly, intimate, and utterly disarming. He kisses her—soft and slow—like it is the first time in years he has wanted a moment to last forever.

By the time Leo enters twenty-three, they are a couple. Quietly, without spectacle. They spend weekends in secondhand bookstores, tracing the shelves with their fingers. They go to obscure film screenings. They take a short trip to the coastal town of Merringdale. Clara keeps a sketchbook of their travels—drawings of Leo playing the piano in the hotel lobby, snippets of things he says without realising how much they reveal.

She grounds him. Not by fixing him, but simply by existing beside him without trying to. She does not ask him to be better. Yet somehow, around her, he wants to be. And for the first time, Leo is not performing love. Neither is he being tortured beneath love's hurricane. He is living it.

But shadows do not vanish just because the room is quiet.

At twenty-four, Leo is shortlisted for a breakthrough initiative for a short film he both wrote and directed. Clara is the first person he calls. Her voice, calm and proud, steadies his nerves like a lullaby. But soon after, as film festivals and meetings start to fill his calendar, the old unease begins to creep in. Not because of Clara. But because of what success dredges up inside him.

There are moments he sees himself slip into charm, into smooth lines, into a persona that wins applause but feels like a betrayal. He hates how natural it still feels. He begins to fear his own voice again.

One afternoon, Clara takes his hand across the table and says, "You do not have to prove anything. Just be here."

Leo swallows hard. For the first time in years, he wants to be seen again. And to be seen—truly seen-is—is to stand still. To stop moving, stop performing. Stillness is something Leo has never learned.

At twenty-five, he relocates to a slightly bigger city, Weltingham, to work on a long-term film project with a respected production house. Clara, meanwhile, takes on a one-year residency at a theatre studio in another town. They try the distance. They send voice notes and train tickets, and pieces of each other's days.

But the quiet of his new apartment is filled with ghosts—old letters, old questions. Not because he is stuck in the past, but because that boy he used to be is still in there somewhere, waiting to be forgiven.

Sometimes Leo wakes up and reaches for Clara beside him, only to remember she is not there. Sometimes, when he hears a particular piece of music, he feels a pang so sharp it almost scares him. Not because he misses Clara. But because he fears losing this, for real. This slow, tender, truthful love that has grown in the quiet corners of his life.

And now, after many years, Leo dares to hope—and makes a decision.

XVI

The House with the Red Door

With trembling hands, Leo pulls open the drawer he has avoided for weeks.

Inside lies his now-battered leather journal—the one constant across the shifting chaos of his years. Its edges are frayed now, corners curling from too many train rides and nights on location. Ink has bled through its pages. A bit of dust smudges his fingertips the moment he touches it. Every mark is a thread in the long fabric of him.

He sits down slowly, as if opening the journal might split him apart.

Within are fragments of a decade: half-songs scrawled between shoots, sleep-starved thoughts penned under weak motel lights, quotes from books he never finished. A list of childhood fears. A confession about his first kiss. Doodles. Coffee rings. Silence.

There are pages about Elise, of course—at first. Dreamlike sketches. Notes she once passed in class.

Snatches of dialogue that haunted him long after their conversations ended. But somewhere toward the endpoint, her presence starts to fade. The ink grows lighter. Then the gaps begin.

And Clara starts appearing in the margins.

Her name slips in like a melody. A sketch of her standing barefoot in a river. A folded paper napkin with her lipstick stain. The word gentle circled three times. A pressed flower. A poem she had murmured and forgotten, but he had written down.

He flips to the very back—and then it appears again, that damned letter to Elise. He stares at it for a long moment. Then, quietly, he slips it out. Folds it once. Twice. Puts it in the drawer meant for things that are never spoken again.

Because as much as he has tried to hate her, he has never stopped needing to protect that part of him that belonged to her. Some wounds deserve their own drawer.

He wraps the rest—the journal, the scribbles, the pressed flower—in plain brown paper. No note. No flourish. Just the hope that Clara might open it and see not a love letter, but a life. A self. A quiet truth.

The train ride to her town is bleak. Rain lashes at the windows with relentless fury. The skies stretch grey across the coast, mirroring the tight knot in his chest. But Leo does not allow himself to overthink. No speeches. No expectations. Just show up.

Clara's street is a little row of homes just off the station—modest, lovely, full of quiet stories. He finds the one she had described—the red door, the lavender bush just beginning to bloom.

He climbs the steps. Heart in his throat.

Raises his hand to knock—

And then stops.

The curtain is not fully drawn.

Through the half-glass, he sees her.

She is barefoot in an oversized jumper, hair tied up in a knot. Laughing. Holding a glass of wine. Soft. Unburdened.

And beside her stands a man.

Not a visitor. Not a fleeting presence.

He pulls something out of the oven. She nudges his side. It is not flirtation—it is rhythm. Intimacy. Familiarity.

And then—

She turns, smiling, hand lifted. And something gleams.

A ring. A band on her finger.

Leo's breath catches.

No. Not like this.

He backs away. Down the steps. Through the hedge.

The parcel in his hand suddenly feels ridiculous. A child's gesture. A play performed in an empty theatre.

He turns the corner. Keeps walking until the house is gone.

He sits on the bench near the station, heart hammering so loudly it sounds like traffic. The parcel lies across his lap like a weight.

He is about to tuck it under his arm and leave when he hears the rattle of a watering can and the shuffle of footsteps on gravel.

An older woman, tending to her potted geraniums by the cafe garden, looks up and offers a genial wave.

"Looks like the rain has eased off a bit, has it not?"

Leo gives a polite nod.

"You visiting someone?" she asks, glancing curiously at the direction he came from.

He hesitates. "Clara."

Her face lights up in recognition. "Ah, Clara Norwood. Everyone knows everyone around here, do not we? She has been through quite a bit, poor girl."

Leo says nothing.

The woman continues, voice dropping to a confiding tone. "Married too young, if you ask me. That first husband of hers... never really fit in. Then one day—gone. And Clara? Vanished not long after. Months passed before anyone saw her again. But she came back, steadier, different somehow. And now she is engaged again. Seems happy. Keeps to herself mostly."

Leo swallows.

The woman gives him a knowing smile. "You a friend?"

He nods faintly.

Then, without another word, he turns and walks away.

On the train back to Weltingham, two schoolboys argue over crisps. A woman complains loudly about her broadband. Somewhere, someone laughs.

Leo does not move.

He watches his reflection in the dark window, split by raindrops and passing lights.

The ache is not loud anymore. It is not theatrical.

It is something else. Still. Hollow. A note that never resolves.

He had thought Clara was the soft place fate owed him. The one untouched by complication.

But maybe life does not owe softness. Maybe it only offers mirrors.

And maybe this one—this cold window, this silence inside—is what karma feels like.

Not dramatic. Not loud.

Just a train ride home.

Soaked to the bone.

No one waiting at the other end.

XVII
The Weight of Quiet Things

It starts slowly.

A missed deadline.

A rewrite that never happens.

A meeting where Leo shows up late, eyes sunken, breath carrying the faint sting of whisky and smoke.

After Clara, something inside him loosens—not in one sharp break, but in a slow, unseen unravelling. Thread by thread, habit by habit.

Days bleed into each other. His apartment in Weltingham grows silent in all the wrong ways. The couch sags with the weight of too many sleepless nights. Half-eaten takeout boxes sit stacked like unfinished thoughts on the counter. Unopened mail collects by the door like autumn leaves, untouched, curling at the edges.

He stops answering calls. He stops returning texts.

He drinks—not socially, not to unwind—but as a means to vanish. Alone, mostly. Always at night. The bottle becomes ritual. It rests beside his keyboard like an old friend who never interrupts.

Work stumbles. Then collapses.

A film he was co-writing falls apart after he misses two crucial meetings and shows up to a third, slurring ideas that made no sense even to him. There is no confrontation. Just a quiet recalibration. A pulled plug. A slow fading out.

And through it all, he pretends.

Pretends that he is thinking. That he is writing. That he is not empty.

Until one afternoon, the phone rings.

The name glows on the screen.

Mum.

He has not spoken to her in weeks.

Not because he meant to disappear, but because he did not know how to explain the void.

He stares at the phone, thumb hovering. He almost lets it go dark.

But something deeper than guilt flickers in his chest. Something old and familiar. The sound of her voice in a childhood fever. The way she once stood outside his locked bathroom door when he was ten and ashamed of crying after a fight with the boys.

He answers.

"Leo?" Her voice is soft, careful as if she is afraid of what she will hear. "Are you alright, love?"

He opens his mouth, but nothing comes out. His throat burns.

There is a pause.

A long one.

Heavy and warm and unbearable.

When he does speak, it is not with words, but a cracked exhale. A sound somewhere between a sigh and a sob.

Something pulled from the quietest part of him.

"Oh, Leo," she murmurs. And in those two syllables, he hears everything: the sleepless nights, the quiet prayers, the ache of not knowing. "I have been so worried. You have not called back. I knew something was wrong."

He wants to lie. To protect her. But the effort is too much.

"Come home," she says gently.

He does not answer.

He just nods, even though she cannot see it—because some part of him, the part that still wants to be saved, has already started packing.

He throws in whatever clothes are clean, tucks his journal inside as well and steps out into the rain.

Riversely greets him with a cloudy sky.

He walks slowly, shoes scuffing against the uneven pavement. There is no rush in his steps—only a heaviness, like he is dragging his regrets behind him.

His house appears at Wesley's, and something shifts in his chest.

His mum opens the door before he knocks.

She is smaller than he remembers. Or maybe it is just the weight of seeing her again through this fog of shame.

She pulls him into a hug without a word, her arms around his back like she is holding the broken pieces of her son together. Leo does not speak. He just closes his eyes and breathes her in.

"Go wash up," she says gently, brushing his hair off his forehead. "You still smell like that awful whisky."

He gives a soft, sheepish smile.

Later, after a warm meal eaten mostly in silence, he wanders to his old room. He sits on the bed, heavy with everything he has not said. The kind of sorrow that does not cry—it just lingers. Lurks.

He opens the window, letting in the cool Riversely air. The smell of rain. Of cut grass. Of familiarity.

Then he walks to the piano and lifts the cover.

The keys are out of tune. His fingers hover, hesitate, then land gently. The notes stumble out, clumsy, unsure—but there.

He plays something. Anything. Just to feel.
And in that quiet room where he once dreamt so many dreams, Leo breaks.
Not loudly.
Not violently.
Just one note at a time.

That night, his mum knocks on the door. He wipes his face and opens it. She does not say anything at first. Just looks at him.

"I am sorry," he whispers. "For worrying you."

She walks in, sits beside him on the bed. "You do not have to apologise for hurting, Leo. But you do have to try. Not for work. Not even for me. For you."

He nods.

It is a long road back. He knows that. But this-this first step, this homecoming—it matters.

In Riversely, under the safety of his mother's roof, Leo sleeps soundly for the first time in days.

And in the morning, when the rain lifts and sunlight starts pouring in, he plays again.

Not for anyone.

Just to hear something beautiful survive inside him.

XVIII
The Roads That Lead Back

The chaos is not loud.
It does not scream or shatter, or break.
It settles. Deep. Quiet. Persistent.

Elise feels it in the way she wakes up before her alarm, the way she presses her fingers to her temples after too much coffee, the way her reflection in the mirror looks composed, competent, yet curiously vacant. Like an unfinished painting—details meticulously rendered, but with something vital left uncoloured.

She tries everything.
She starts waking up earlier, as if discipline might carve out clarity.
She runs through misty streets before the world stirs, pounding pavement as though she can outrun the restlessness in her ribs. But when she stops, breathless and burning, the feeling is still there.

She books herself into wellness retreats, tucked in places with herbal teas, quiet chants, and softly spoken mantras. She practices silence. Journals. Eats clean. A stranger presses stones to her spine and tells her to let go of what no longer serves her.

She tries yoga. Seated on dewy grass at sunrise, surrounded by people humming intentions into the morning. She folds herself into child's pose and hopes the quiet will stretch into her bones.

For a while, it works. Or seems to.

She breathes deeper. Smiles a bit. Tells herself healing is linear.

But at night, when she closes her eyes, it returns—
The ache.
The absence.
The unanswered question that no mantra has yet silenced.

She tries dating again—tentatively, half-heartedly.

A historian with a mind as sharp as a blade, who speaks about the past like it is still happening. A journalist with ink-stained fingers, who laughs easily and writes her poems on napkins.

And yet, always the same cycle.

The excitement, the flicker of possibility.
The growing weariness.
The inevitable fading.

Elise already knows: the problem is not them. If it never was.

The wine bottles on her windowsill grow in number. The books she buys go unread. She rearranges furniture, repaints a wall, throws herself into projects with a feverish intensity that does not feel like passion, but distraction.

Still, the question lingers, heavy and unanswered:

What is missing?

One evening, standing at her window, she realises she already knows the answer.

Not a place. Not a person.

But something buried deep in her past—

Some part of herself she has left behind. Something she needs to recover and bring back with her.

And so, one Friday night, after another fruitless attempt at finding solace in a city that never quite felt like home, she books a train ticket.

To Riversely.

She arrives just as the first threads of sunlight stretch across the sky. Riversely is still. The streets breathe in the soft hush of morning, shop shutters still drawn, the air carrying the faint scent of damp earth and fresh bread.

Elise does not go straight home.

She walks first. Through the town she once knew so intimately. Past Calloway's, past Wren & Quill, and past the riverbank, where she recalls teenage versions of herself and Leo sitting side by side, arguing about whether architects or filmmakers shaped the world more. Past the school gates of Riversely High, standing as solid and unchanged as a memory frozen in time.

Then, at last, home.

The house feels smaller than she remembers. Or maybe she has just grown.

Her mother greets her with a sleepy hug and a pot of coffee brewing on the stove. There is no grand reunion, no dramatic moment—just warmth, the kind that does not need to be spoken. Elise drops her suitcase in her room, picks up a mug of coffee from her childhood kitchen, and lets the familiarity of home seep into her bones.

And then—

Somewhere in the quiet of morning, she hears it.

A piano.

A song she knows.

She stills, heart tightening, the mug halfway to her lips.

It is coming from across the lane. From the house she knows as well as her own.

The notes are slow, deliberate, a tune woven with thought rather than habit. A melody she has not heard in years but recognises in an instant.

She sets the mug down.

Without thinking, without questioning, she moves. Slips into her shoes and coat, picks up her handbag, pushes open the door, and steps out into the chilly morning air.

The music pulls her forward, like a thread tugging her back through time.

And as she reaches the familiar gate, her breath catches.

Because behind the window pane, sitting at the piano, his head bowed, fingers drifting over the keys—

Is Leo.

Elise does not breathe for a moment.

She just stands there, hidden slightly by the fence, watching him as if she has stumbled into a dream stitched from memory and longing. The morning light spills through the half-open window, catching the curve of his cheek, the fall of his brown hair, the stillness in his posture that seems so unlike the Leo she once knew.

But it is him. And then, just like that, he stops playing.

The final note fades like a sigh, and he turns.

His eyes find her through the open window. They widen, just slightly. No surprise. Just something raw and unguarded, as though he, too, had been haunted by this possibility and now was not sure if it was real.

He stands slowly, pushing the stool back. A moment passes—long and uncertain—before he walks over to the front door and opens it fully.

"Elise," he says, her name like a question and an answer all at once.

She steps forward, cautiously, the gravel crunching underfoot. She does not know what she expected—a greeting, an excited laugh, anger? But what she sees in his eyes is not either. It is weariness. It is the weight of everything unspoken.

For a second, they just stand there, the silence dense around them.

He opens the door wider.

"Come in," he says quietly.

She does.

Inside, the Whitmore house is exactly as Elise remembers. The same floral curtains Leo's mother always favoured—sun-faded now, but still fluttering like old habits. The photo wall near the stairs is cluttered with crooked frames and frozen smiles, some askew as though the laughter inside them never quite settled.

The scent of warm tea lingers beneath something faintly citrus, maybe the remains of a lemon cake or the hand soap in the kitchen. There are books balanced on armrests, half-folded blankets on the sofa, and a pair of Leo's trainers kicked under the hallway bench.

She seeps in everything slowly when a voice startles her. From the kitchen, Marion Whitmore turns and gasps softly. Her face lights up with a mixture of joy and disbelief. "Elise? Oh, oh, sweetheart, is that really you?"

Elise manages a smile. "Hello, Marion."

The older woman crosses the space and hugs her tightly, the kind of embrace that makes Elise close her eyes, if only to hold back the sudden sting. It feels safe. It feels undeserved.

Marion pulls back, but her smile wavers when she turns to Leo. She sees it—whatever it is Elise saw in the music, in the silence. That dullness behind his eyes. That lack of light.

"I am still worried about you," she murmurs to him.

He does not answer. Just nods faintly.

And Marion, in her quiet wisdom, touches Elise's arm and says gently, "I have got errands in town. Might take the whole day, truth be told." She does not look at either of them when she adds, "The house could use a little music again."

Then she is gone, the door clicking shut behind her.

They are alone.

Leo turns to Elise. There is a beat of quiet, heavy and long, before he says, "Do you want to come to my room?"

She nods. It is the only thing she can manage.

The short walk is a slow echo of a thousand memories. Her hand brushes the walls as it once did when they were thirteen, laughing too loud, running too fast. Now, there is no laughter. Only silence stretching between them like a thread not yet broken.

His room has not changed much.

Books still line the walls, though they are even more disorganised now. Piano notes are scattered across his desk—some scribbled hastily, others so smudged they are barely legible. There is a worn armchair by the window, a blanket slung carelessly across it. And the air smells like rain on wood and faint cologne and something Elise can only describe as Leo.

He gestures for her to sit. She does not. She stays near the door, arms folded, as if unsure whether this is truly happening.

He speaks first.

"I did not think you would ever come back here."

She swallows. "I did not think you would still be here to come back to."

His mouth lifts at the corner, but it is not quite a smile. "Thought about leaving. Thought about a lot of things."

There is a pause.

"Your call," she says suddenly. "That night."

Leo looks up, startled.

She folds her arms tighter. "You were drunk. You said things I did not understand. Then you hung up. And I—"

She stops. The words crumble at the edge.

He leans back against the desk, head tilted slightly. He knows it is Elise. Hasty, confronting, speaking what is on her mind—fast—always too fast. He smiles at the realisation and simply replies, "I was... lost. I did not have any answers then. I barely have them now."

Silence again.

And then he adds, voice lower: "I hurt a lot of people trying to figure myself out. But I never meant to hurt you."

She closes her eyes.

He steps closer. Not too close. Just enough that she can hear the catch in his breath when he says, "I never gave you a real chance to see me, Elise. And maybe you never wanted to. But even back then—" his voice falters "—you were the only one who ever could."

She looks at him.

Tired, hollow, still brilliant. Still, the boy who once played piano like it was his soul speaking. But now, there is something new: a quiet man, stripped bare of illusions, trying to find himself in the ruins.

And Elise does not know what it means yet. Does not know what she wants to ask or offer.

But she is here.

And that, for now, is enough.

He gestures toward the piano. "Would you mind if I...?"

She shakes her head.

He sits again, places his fingers on the keys. A new melody this time. Unfinished, aching, searching.

• 95 •

Elise sinks into the armchair and listens.

The room is silent except for the piano, and the way it seems to speak in a language that no one else can hear. Leo does not look at her. He does not need to. His fingers are telling the story—of years passed, of nights lost, of everything that had no name.

The music is not perfect. It stumbles, pauses, gasps for breath. But it is honest. It is real. Like an old wound aired out after years beneath bandages.

She watches him, not as the boy she once knew, but as something else entirely—someone worn down by time, by memory, by something she can't quite name. He is at once a stranger and the most familiar thing in her world.

When he finishes, he does not speak. The room hangs in silence, full of things neither of them know how to say.

Then: "Would you mind playing with me?" he asks, eyes still on the keys.

Elise lets out a breath. "I do not know how."

Leo turns to her, and in that one moment, something shifts between them—something vast and unseen, shifting far below the surface.

"Then I will teach you," he says quietly.

She stands slowly, her limbs unsure. The floorboards creak beneath her feet as she crosses the room. The space beside him on the bench is narrow, their arms pressed lightly together. Warmth bleeds through fabric. Neither moves away.

He lifts her hand, carefully, and places her fingers on the keys. "Start here."

Her touch is clumsy. The sound jars. She laughs, half embarrassed, half vulnerable.

But Leo only smiles. "Again."

He guides her fingers, gently. Their hands brush—once, twice—and neither pulls back. The melody begins to form, halting but tender, like two people relearning how to speak in a shared voice.

He leans closer, just enough for her to feel his breath. "Do not think. Just follow the sound."

They play like that for a while—her following, him leading—until the notes seem to find their own rhythm, low and soft, echoing around the room like a whisper of something long forgotten.

When the music fades, she does not move. Neither does he.

There is a silence now that feels fuller than sound.

Elise turns to him slowly, eyes searching his face. "Why did you cut all contact with me?"

Leo does not flinch. His voice, when it comes, is quiet. "Because I was angry at you for leaving me behind. You recall that letter?"

She does not respond.

He looks at her then—really looks. Her eyes are tired. Older. But something in them still glows faintly, like the last ember in a dying fire.

And then, without quite meaning to, she shifts closer. Not much. Just enough for her knee to brush his.

Leo does not ask why. He does not speak. He simply lifts one arm—an unspoken invitation.

Elise slides in, rests her head against his chest, and wraps both arms around him.

For a second, he freezes—then his other arm folds around her, pulling her in tighter.

He buries his face in her hair, breathing her in. She smells faintly of turpentine and rosewater, like ink stains and evening light.

Their first real hug. Their full, sinking-into-each-other kind of embrace.

She presses her face to his shoulder, and suddenly, the world stills. The noise quiets.

For Elise, it is like falling into a memory she never knew she needed. His warmth, his scent—faintly of old paper and the citrus soap he never changes—wrap around her like a blanket after a long storm. Her chest aches. Her eyes sting. She had not realised how much she missed being held like this. Not just held, but seen. Safe. It makes her feel alive again—therapeutic, healing in a way she had forgotten was possible.

For a moment, the noise quiets. The questions, the ache, the heaviness—vanish. In his arms, everything feels lighter. As if the world, just briefly, remembers how to be kind.

For Leo, it is something else entirely. A letting go. His fingers curl into the back of her jumper, and he breathes her in like she is the only clean air in his cluttered world. With her in his arms, the noise in his head quiets for the first time in months. The tension in his jaw, the weight in his spine—it all melts into her. She is gravity and balm and gravity again.

And they do not let go.
If anything, they hold on tighter.

Something settles.
Something returns.

And then—
Without thinking, without shattering the silence, they kiss.

And it shifts everything.

Their lips meet like notes in the same key—two sounds made to echo together. There is no hesitation. Only familiarity, and something that trembles just beneath the surface. Something deep like the ocean. Strange even. A recognition that defies definition.

His hands find her waist.

Hers tangle in his hair.

They rise together from the piano bench, slowly, without a word.

Clothes fall quietly to the floor, like the shedding of old selves.

He lays her down on the bed, the one he once dreamed of her in, the one she never thought she'd return to. Now, here they are—not rewriting history, but folding it into the present.

Their bodies move in rhythm, not with urgency, but with reverence. A search. A return. A breath drawn in tandem.

He studies the curve of her neck, the flicker of her lashes, the way she gasps when he touches the place just above her hip. She traces the scar on his shoulder with her lips, tastes the years between them on his skin.

Passion hums beneath them—undeniable.

Forgiveness lingers in the space between them, gentle as breath.

But what exists between them now is something quieter. Deeper.

A kind of recognition.

Like standing before a mirror and seeing not only your own reflection—but everything you have lost, and everything you never realised you were waiting for.

When they arrive at that unspoken place, it does not feel like a climax.

It feels like convergence.

A stillness heavier than sound.

A silence that says, we are here.

Afterwards, they lie entangled beneath the thin duvet, barely touching, and yet unable to part.

The room smells of something ancient—memory and breath and skin and hope.

Elise stares at the ceiling. Her heart is not racing. It is beating slowly, deeply, like it is trying to tell her something she cannot quite understand.

Leo lies beside her, eyes open, staring into nowhere in particular.

Neither speaks for a long time.

And then she says, very quietly, "What is this?"

He exhales. "I do not know. Not really."

But he thinks to himself:

It is not love—not the kind either he or she has known.
It is not longing, either.

It is something older, quieter. A knowing without needing.
Like recognising your own breath in another body.

It is a question, still unfolding.
A truth he has no language for.
Not yet.

But it is real. And perhaps, far greater than love, as if their souls have always lived in parallel, and this moment is where the lines finally touch.

XIX

When Silence Breathes Your Name

Then Leo shifts, just enough that his voice brushes the edge of her skin. "I used to think pain had to be loud to be real."

She does not move. Just listens.

"But it turns out... sometimes it is the quiet that ruins you."

His thumb traces the inside of her wrist slowly, like he is mapping memories into her.

"I met someone. Clara." The name lands between them like a small stone. "She was kind. Steady. Nothing like the chaos I had come from. She saw me—but maybe only the part I was trying to be. And I..." He swallows. "I thought maybe that was enough."

Elise turns to look at him, her cheek against the pillow. She says nothing.

"She was already married, and then, she got engaged to someone else," he says after a pause, his voice rough. "And I did not know. I was ready to give her everything. My story. Even that stupid old journal."

There is a flicker of pain across his face, sharp and sudden. "And then I saw her with him. And it was like..." He falters. "Like the last piece of me that still believed in clean chances just cracked."

He reaches down and pulls his old bag from beneath the bed, unzips it slowly, and takes out the journal—soft-edged, worn, its spine tired from years of opening and closing.

"I was going to give it to her," he says quietly. "I thought she would understand me."

A beat passes, then he looks at her. "But it was always meant to be yours, was not it?"

Elise does not answer right away. She just watches as he holds it out.

"I want you to have it," he says. "And if there are still pages left... maybe you can finish them. With your thoughts. If you want to. I have nothing left to write, really."

Elise nods, silent, and takes the journal with both hands. She opens her handbag and places it inside carefully, as though it is made of something breakable.

Then she reaches for his hand. She does not speak. She does not need to. She offers no sympathy either—only space.

A place for his hurt to land and still be safe.

He exhales slowly. "I do not know who I am anymore. But this morning... this silence with you... it scares me even more."

A long pause. Then, softly: "Are you hungry?"

Elise lifts a brow. "Is that your way of changing the subject?"

He smiles, the corner of his mouth tugging like it remembers laughter. "It is my way of feeding the only person who has managed to look at me like I am not broken." "Okay then, I will cook," she says, wondering how she is hungry again—all of a sudden—after all these months.

She rises, the bedsheet falling from her as she stretches. She picks up one of his shirts from the chair beside the bed and puts it on. "Mum just washed it, Marlowe. Had you asked, I would have lent you one from the pile kept for laundry," Leo teases her. "Consider yourself lucky, Whitmore, your shirt will thank you later," she snaps.

The shirt hangs loosely on her bare thighs, the hem brushing mid-leg, buttons undone just enough to reveal the soft curve of her collarbone. Sunlight spills in behind her, turning her hair into ribbons of gold and shadow.

He stares.

Not with lust. Not first.

With awe.

Because there is something devastatingly honest about her—standing in his shirt, barefoot on the wooden floor, hair a little wild, face unpainted, eyes holding years.

And somehow, she is the most beautiful thing he has ever seen.

She wanders into the kitchen and starts pulling things from the cabinets like she has been there forever. Leo follows, leans against the counter, watches her crack eggs into a bowl, fingers nimble, casual. She hums under her breath—an old song he once played, years ago. She remembers.

He steps closer. Close enough to feel her warmth again.

"I never told you," he murmurs, his voice brushing against the back of her neck, "How often I imagined this.

Just you. In my shirt. Making eggs in the quiet of some morning."

Elise glances over her shoulder. "You imagined eggs?"

"You won't change, will you, idiot. I imagined *you*," he says.

And that is all it takes.

She turns. The bowl is forgotten, the air between them thick with something unspoken, undeniable. He steps in, hands reaching for her face with reverence. Their mouths meet again—this time faster, heavier, full of the ache of everything unsaid.

He lifts her onto the counter.

The sunlight kisses her thighs, the hem of his shirt sliding higher with each breath. She pulls him in, fingers curling into his hair, and this time, there is nothing cautious. No restraint. Only a long-held tension, finally allowed to unravel.

They move together as if they were made for it—not in heat, but in hunger. The hunger to be seen, to be known, to be held in a way the world never allows.

He studies her skin like it holds answers—tracing every freckle, every scar, every dip of bone and breath. She explores him like a map she once knew but had lost the language for.

Her hands slide beneath his shirt, splaying across his back, grounding him. His breath stutters as she presses her lips to his throat, to the place beneath his ear, to the place where grief still lingers in muscle memory.

There is nothing performative in this.

No script.

Just sensation. Two bodies remembering what their souls already knew.

When it is over, they stay where they are. His forehead pressed to hers. Their breaths syncing. Her legs wrapped around his waist like she is afraid to let go.

He brushes a strand of hair from her cheek.

She studies his face—every crack and line, the quiet sadness that has lived there too long.

"What are *we*?" she asks again, voice raw, barely above a whisper.

He does not answer. But this time, he knows—for sure: this collision of memory and flesh—it is not an accident. It is not a mistake.

And as the morning sun climbs higher, casting soft gold across their skin, he realises:

Elise can never be one of his chapters.
She is the footnote in every line he has ever written.
She is the book he keeps returning to—and will always.

But does Elise realise it yet? He needs to know—from her.

Leo glances at her, half-draped in his shirt, her knees drawn up on the sofa, mug of tea and a plate of toast and scrambled eggs balanced between her palms. The late morning light slides through the curtains in soft waves, and in this quiet, lived-in calm, she looks like something out of memory. Out of something deeper than that, even—something closer to the soul.

He wants to ask her.

Wants to reach across the small space between them and say, 'See me.'

But he knows Elise. He knows the way she builds walls. Out of self-preservation and sometimes, untold spite. He knows the pride that hides her softness. And he knows—if he wants her truth, he must be patient enough to let it come.

He says nothing. Just watches her quietly, the way he always has.

Eventually, she exhales. A long, slow breath like something heavy is finally loosening its grip.

"I have changed, Leo."

Her voice is quiet. Not uncertain—just... careful.

"I do not think I am who I used to be. And not in that poetic, growth kind of way. I mean—really changed."

She keeps her eyes on the tea, as if it is safer than looking at him.

"There were men. After Daniel. After everything. I thought I loved them. I did the things people do when they are trying to move on. I laughed, I slept beside them, I built futures in my head. I even told myself I was healed."

She gives a small laugh, dry and hollow.

"But I never really was."

Leo listens. His chest aches, but he lets her speak. He owes her that. He owes her everything.

"I always left," she continues. "Eventually. Sometimes with reason, sometimes just... because. Something always felt wrong. Or missing. Or off. And I would tell myself it was about timing, or incompatibility, or whatever convenient excuse I needed that week."

Her fingers tighten slightly around the mug.

"But the truth is—maybe I am not meant to love someone. Maybe I do not know how. Or maybe I am incapable of giving the kind of love people seem to need from me."

She looks up at him then. Really looks. Eyes wide and open, like she is bracing for something—judgement, disappointment, maybe even pity.

But Leo does not flinch.

His gaze is steady. Soft. Because how could he ever judge the girl who once gave him the sky with a piano melody and a secret smile?

And yet—his heart pulls taut.

He wants to scream, *it is not that you cannot love—it is that you already did.*
You have already loved someone so much, no one else has ever stood a chance. Damn it, why cannot you see? Are you that stupid with that brilliant brain of yours?

But he does not say any of that.

Instead, he nods gently. He shifts just enough to be closer, their knees brushing now.

"I think," she continues carefully, "Some people are not meant to find love the way others do. Some of us do not fall in love—we collide with it. And after that...nothing feels quite real again."

She swallows, blinking.

"I do not know what I am looking for," she whispers.

You are looking for us, he thinks.
You are looking for the thing we had before we even understood what it was.
Before the world came in and pulled us into different orbits.

But he does not say that either.

Instead, he leans his head back against the sofa and sighs. "It is okay not to know. You will know when you do."

And he means it.

He has changed, too. He is no longer the boy impatient for answers, for promises.
He can wait.

Or so he tells himself.

Because what he feels for Elise is not urgency. It is not desperation.
It is something quieter. Fiercer. Truer.

It is devotion, without demand. Worship even.

And so, they sit like that.

Two people not quite broken, but not whole either.

Curled into the soft ache of each other's presence.

Outside, the day unfolds slowly—birds chirp without drama, the wind rustles dry leaves, and somewhere, a neighbour's dog barks at the sun.

Inside, there are no confessions. No promises. No declarations.

Only the quiet knowing of two souls who once exchanged something deeper than love.

Something that has not faded.

Something that waits.

Still. Maybe...

XX

Some Goodbyes Do Not Echo

The afternoon spills into a lazy golden haze.

They sit in the garden, munching on fish and chips that he had ordered, talking about everything and nothing—childhood dares, failed school projects, teachers with odd mannerisms, old bikes, old friends. Elise laughs more than she has in weeks. Her voice rings out across the backyard like a familiar song, and Leo drinks it in like a man lost in a desert, finding a spring he did not think existed anymore.

And as the light slants across the blooms, Elise begins to notice it again. That quiet thing about Leo. But it is not the same. Back then, in their teens, his quiet was a secret thing, something only she could see—hidden beneath the wild, charming boy the world thought they knew. A quietness, reserved just for her, like a soft chord only she could hear.

Now, he is silent, almost all the time. Composed. Steady. As if it has become his habit, his second nature. As if life has pressed pause on that boy he used to be and replaced him with someone older, less open, less ablaze. That fire he carried—the reckless laughter, the midnight spontaneity—feels far away now. Extinguished, or maybe just buried.

He is still handsome. She had known it even back then. But now, there is a gravity to him. A kind of ache stitched into the way he carries himself.

She does not realise the way he looks at her, too, how the sun catches in her chestnut hair, how her cheekbones cast delicate shadows when she turns, how the curve of her frame still holds a kind of effortless elegance. She is slender but strong, worn at the edges in the way beautiful things are when they have survived.

He catches her watching once, and she looks away too fast. Laughs at something that was not funny, just to break the weight of the moment.

As the sun dips lower and the evening air cools, the weight returns. She glances at her phone and sighs. "I should go soon. I only took the day off. There is a team meeting tomorrow evening."

Something deflates in Leo.

He nods, even as every part of him wants to say *stay*. Or—at least—*come back soon*.

But she is already on her feet, brushing invisible creases from her jeans and adjusting the strap of her bag. He follows her inside. She picks up her coat from the hallway, slinging it over her shoulder.

There is a silence as he walks her to the door. A moment with too many unspoken things straining against the edges.

And then, she starts rambling.

"I think... I think I just need to focus on my work right now," she says, adjusting her coat. "I have wasted so much time chasing... illusions. Maybe I am just not meant for any of that. Love. Or whatever people call it. It does not seem to work with me."

She offers a short laugh, but it is brittle. Forced.

"I always end up disappointed. Or disappointing someone. So maybe I am better off keeping it simple. Focused. I know who I am when I work. I do not, when I am—when I am around people like that."

Leo watches her. Every word slices cleaner than the last.

People like that. People who want to stay. People who see her. People like... *him.*

He opens his mouth, a gentle *what if we were in the same city* forming on his tongue, but swallows it. She has already convinced herself. Already closed the door before he could knock.

And just like that, she is gone.

The door clicks softly behind her. She does not look back.

Leo stands for a moment in the quiet house, her scent still lingering in the hallway, his shirt still clinging to the ghost of her shape. And the ache, the old, slow ache that once dragged him, returns.

But this is different.

This is not betrayal.

This is not heartbreak.

This is something worse.

This is invisibility.

She did not see it.

Even now, after everything, she still does not see him.

Just like the letter at the ball.

And he had thought—foolishly—that this time would be different. That maybe, in the quiet of shared spaces and familiar silences, she would look at him and finally know.

But Elise is not ready.

Or maybe, worse—she never will be.

And suddenly, waiting feels too dangerous.

Because Leo knows her.

He knows how her heart sways like wind on glass—brilliant, impulsive, always reaching for something just beyond.

She disappears without warning. Builds bridges, then burns them by moonlight.

And perhaps, more than anything, she won't face the truth—not because she cannot see it, but because she will only believe what she tells herself.

Stubborn in silence. Adamant in her own weather.

Leo knows himself, too. He knows what Elise means to him.

And if he waits again—if he dares to hope again—only to find her gone, or indifferent, or chasing a kind of love that was never meant to stay—

It will kill him.

Not all at once.

But slowly. Quietly.

Like a thread being pulled from the inside, unravelling every soft part of him.

He won't let that happen.

So, he makes a decision.

Before the night thickens, before she can return in the morning to say her goodbyes with polite smiles and that flare in her addictive eyes, he packs his bag. Quietly. Methodically. With the same numbness, one uses to bandage a wound that has not bled yet. He carefully folds the shirt she had worn, pausing for a moment, fingers brushing over the faint imprint of her, then places it inside his bag like it is something sacred.

He leaves a letter on the kitchen counter for his mum.

"Do not worry. I just needed to be elsewhere. I will call. Love you always."

Then he walks down the garden path, past the window where Elise had once stood watching him play the piano, past the ghosts of laughter that still live in the walls.

He boards the train just after midnight. No crowd. No sound.

As the train pulls away from Riversely, Leo stares out into the dark.

And then—quietly—he blocks Elise's number.

He knows what he is doing.

He is not punishing her.

He is protecting himself.

Because this is not a story anymore.

This is not a song.

This is the silence between verses.

And he does not know what comes next.

But he knows—he cannot bear to keep re-reading a chapter that never changes.

Morning comes with the soft grey hush of a Riversely dawn. Mist hugs the fields. The hedges drip with dew. The town still sleeps.

Elise folds her clothes with deliberate care, as if the neatness of her packing might tame the chaos swelling in her chest. There is a heaviness in her limbs this morning, a weight that settled in her bones sometime between his touch and her own declarations the previous day.

I cannot love.

She had said *it*. Loud enough for him to hear, perhaps even for herself. And yet, after all that—after the stillness of the previous morning, his arms around her, the way his heartbeat matched hers like a secret rhythm—it felt false now. Like armour, she was not sure she needed any more, but was not brave enough to remove.

She zips up her suitcase. Takes one last look at her room. Leo's scent still lingers faintly in her skin. And then, she brushes her hair, fixes her lipstick, and steps out with a strange flutter in her chest. Nervousness. Anticipation. The fragile hope of a shared breakfast, maybe. A warm cup of tea. A soft smile exchanged. Some wordless promise that this—whatever this was—was not just a dream.

She reaches his house, her boots crunching over the familiar path.

The gate squeaks the same. The windows catch the same morning light.

But something is...off.

Too still.

She knocks. Once. Twice. Presses the bell.

Nothing.

Her brows furrow. She calls out softly, "Leo?"

Still nothing.

The door remains closed, silent as stone.

She walks around to the back, peeks into the garden, and into the kitchen windows. The kettle is not on. His mug is not on the counter. There are no shoes in the hall. Not a trace of movement.

Marion had not returned last night, and Leo…

Gone.

Elise blinks.

She tries calling him.

One ring. Two. Call failed.

She frowns. Tries again. Same thing.

Pulling her phone closer, she stares at the screen. And then, it hits her.

You have been blocked.

Her hand freezes.

Her breath stops.

For a long moment, she stands still—absolutely still—like the universe itself has just gone out of alignment.

Blocked.

Blocked. Blocked.

She laughs then. A hollow sound, echoing in the empty air.

"Unbelievable," she mutters, stepping back.

Of course. It is Leo. Brilliant at disappearing. Slipping out of life the way a dream fades, the moment you try to hold onto it.

Anger rushes in, hot and sharp. "Coward," she spits under her breath. "After everything, you run? Again?"

Her pulse is thudding now, her cheeks burning.

He left.

After last night. After that music. After that touch. That silence between them that said more than words.

He just *left.*

Did not even say goodbye.

Did not trust her enough to say it in person.

And the worst part—the part she won't admit even to herself—is the betrayal wrapped in the fear.

Because somewhere beneath the fire of her fury is a chill.

What if he did not mean any of it?

What if everything she felt last night—everything she thought he felt—was just... a moment for him? Temporary. Replaceable. Like one of his scripts—just another storyline, another subject he had explored and abandoned.

What if it was his way of punishing her quietly?

Her doubts creep up again, dragging with them the weight of old memories—of not knowing where she truly stood in the theatre of his life, of thinking she knew him but never quite able to peer deep enough into his mind.

She feels something crack deep inside her. The old wound. The one she thought had healed. The one she had buried under career goals and clever distractions.

"No," she says aloud. "Screw this."

She opens her phone.

Scrolls.

Finds his name.

Presses *block*.

There. Done. Equal now.

"Hell with him."

And yet, the words taste bitter.

There is a thin film of tears threatening behind her eyes, but she blinks them away. She won't cry for him. Not Leo. Not again.

She turns around, jaw clenched, and walks down the path. Does not look back at the house. Does not glance at the window where she once watched him play the piano. Does not give herself the chance to feel anything else.

She walks to the station with her chin high, like a woman who has made up her mind.

But on the train, when the landscape starts to blur past her window and the fog begins to lift, something inside her clenches—something she cannot name.

A hollow where something just used to be.

And as she rests her head against the glass, arms folded, breath shaky, Elise tells herself she is done with him.

For good.

But even now, even as the train carries her away from Riversely—she wonders if she is really blocking Leo...

Or just trying to silence something in herself that refuses to stop calling his name.

XXI
Unnamed Ghosts

Weltingham greets Leo, soulless. He steps into his flat with the quiet finality of someone closing a door behind a memory. The silence inside feels loud. Deafening.

The first few days, he keeps himself busy. Emails. Deadlines. Edits. Long walks to nowhere. He tells himself this was the right thing. *She* never saw him. Even when he stood in front of her, hands trembling from loving her too much, she chose to ramble about independence and solitude like a shield she never learned to put down.

So he had blocked her. And he had told himself—*done.*

But then the dreams begin.

At first, they are vague. Disjointed images. The swing in her garden, creaking in the wind. The smell of turpentine on her fingers. Her voice saying, *"I never could sleep in silence."*

Then it gets worse.

He sees her walking barefoot in snow, blood trailing behind her, staining white into red. Sometimes she is herself clad in white—drenched, eyes wide, wrists cut. He rushes to hold her, but she crumbles like ash.

Sometimes it is Isla. A night in the lake. But when she turns, her eyes are Elise's. And she says, *"You left me, too."*

He jolts awake, drenched in sweat. He does not sleep again that night.

And the dreams get darker.

They are back in his childhood bedroom, candlelight flickering against the ceiling. She is in his shirt again—that shirt—but her body is covered in bruises he never gave.

He tries to touch her, and her skin splits open, showing a ribcage with his name carved into it.

Other nights, it is their lovemaking on loop. But warped. Like a reel replaying on broken film. He touches her, and she whispers, *"You' will never be enough."*

He starts hating her. Not really. But the *idea* of her. The Elise that burned herself into his synapses rewrote his very biology. The Elise who bled chaos into his ordered world and then left.

She planted a hurricane inside him, kissed him while the storm surged, and then walked away like it was just weather.

He tries dating again. Once. A kind editor named Elsa, but fate loves a cruel rhyme. She touches his wrist over dinner, and he flinches like he has been burned.

He deletes her number before he reaches home.

He stops playing again–and this time, it seems to be forever. He stops listening to music altogether. Anything with chords hurts. Especially the unresolved ones.

Work loses flavour. Food tastes like ash. Days blend.

He opens a bottle of scotch one night and finishes it in silence. Then another. It has become a habit.

He stops calling his mother again.

His world shrinks. The flat becomes a cave.

But it is not Elise's absence that hurts most—it is the knowing that if she had asked him to stay, if she had just looked at him differently, he would would thrown away everything.

That is what terrifies him. That some connections could be so unhinged, and yet, so absolute.

And then, it happens.

One night, he stands on the edge of the riverbank—the waters, black and wide, beckoning.

He closes his eyes.

He thinks of nothing. And then—Isla. Standing on the edge, waiting for him, but he never came. Her scream still lives somewhere inside his lungs.

Then he sees another face—his mother. Her hands that once held his face when he cried. Her voice: *"Please do not leave me too."*

He steps back. Breath hitching.

His feet are still on land.

That is the night he realises he needs professional help.

XXII

Sylvia, in Stillness

It is raining the next morning. The city glistens with cold silver. A taxi drops Leo outside a private mental health centre tucked behind a garden that smells of wet leaves and old stone. The receptionist looks up, startled by his drenched coat and hollow face. He has nothing on him but his phone and a credit card.

Leo does not talk much on that first day. He just signs the forms, agrees to a short stay, and follows a nurse to a quiet room with pale walls and an empty chair by the window. There is a view of a lane in the distance—dark, winding, almost mythical in how it waits.

He sleeps for almost fourteen hours.
And when he wakes, it is Sylvia.

She walks in quietly, holding a leather notebook and a cup of mint tea she never offers. She does not introduce herself like a saviour, only sits across from him and says, "I am not here to fix you. But I will sit with you while you break."

Leo watches her. She is in her early late twenties. Her hair is brown and pinned back loosely, no makeup, no pretense. There is something in the way she occupies space—gentle but immovable. Like moss after rain. Still. Absorbing.

He does not speak in the first session. Neither does she, much. Only a few questions—name, medication history, whether he has slept. At the end, she says softly, "You do not have to speak until your silence begins to ache."

It takes five sessions.

On the sixth, he says, "I almost jumped."

Sylvia does not blink. She only nods. "And then?"

Leo looks at the wall. His voice is paper. "Then I saw her face. Isla's. And my mum's. And then I could not."

The sessions become a ritual. She never pushes too hard. Never lets him spiral too deep. There are days when he shows up furious, pacing, blaming *someone* he knows too well in metaphors. Other days, he is quiet. Numb. She never lets him deflect for long. When he rambles about work or the news, she stops him with a look and a single word: "Pause."

He begins to call her *'the anchor'*. Not to her face. Only in his head.

And yet—he cannot say Elise's name. Not once.

Sylvia notices. Of course, she does. In one session, she simply asks, "What are you avoiding?"

Leo scoffs. "I am not."

"What is actually bothering you so much?"

He goes still. The silence that follows feels endless. Then he says, "I cannot."

She nods. "That is okay. We will wait for it."

Over time, Sylvia's presence becomes its own language. She listens without absorbing his pain, yet it is clear she carries the weight of her work like stone in her coat pockets. Leo begins noticing the way her eyes soften when he talks about Isla. The way she closes her notebook when something hurts him. She is never performative. Never warm to please. Her warmth is earned. Quiet.

He starts looking forward to the sessions. Then, dreading the end of them.

One day, he opens up about Clara. Slowly. Like spitting out pieces of broken glass.

"She lied," he says one day, eyes fixed on the carpet. "Said she loved me."

Sylvia listens, still as ever.

"She was not," Leo continues... "Married as a teen. A whole life elsewhere. A husband. Then, a fiance. Everything. I was the escape hatch." His laugh is bitter. "I was the secret."

Sylvia does not interrupt. Just lets the words unravel.

After he finishes, there is a long silence. The kind that weighs.

Then Sylvia says, with quiet certainty, "That was not love, Leo. That was something to fill the void within you."

He nods slowly. "I keep wondering why I attract people who leave."

"You do not," she says gently. "You just keep giving your light to those who do not know how to carry it."

He tells her about the boy he used to be. The one who played music because it saved him. She asks gently, "And now?"

Leo's voice cracks. "Now I cannot touch the keys."

She lets the silence stretch.

Then says, "One day, you will."

It is not until much later, after months, that something begins to shift. He is sitting across from her, watching the way she tucks a loose strand of hair behind her ear, and the realisation crawls up his throat like a warning:

He cares.

Not the way he did for Elise. Those emotions were thunder. Wild and devouring. This—this is the space after storms. The hush. The clearing.

He panics. Misses two sessions. Then calls.

She does not scold. Does not interpret. Only says, "I wondered if you had run."

His voice is quiet. "I did."

"Did it help?"

"No."

They do not speak of love. Not yet. But she slowly stops being his therapist. Passes him on to another. Keeps her distance. Still meets him for tea in the garden, though. They speak of poems. Silence. Music. She never touches him.

And somehow, that devastates him more than anything else.

She is the calm after Elise. The woman who shows him he can be known, wholly, and still be safe.

XXIII
The Ache of
Beautiful Things

From the outside, Elise Marlowe is thriving.

She speaks at panels, her essays appear in architectural journals across Europe, her designs are shortlisted for international awards. Her inbox is overflowing. Colleagues call her formidable. She smiles on red carpets, holds champagne flutes without spilling a drop. Her posture says confidence. Her voice never shakes.

She is twenty eight and luminous.

And yet—something has gone quiet inside her.

The shift is gradual.

Conversations bore her. Dinners feel like formalities. She dates men—kind, intelligent, often well-read—but they all feel like silhouettes. She kisses them and feels nothing. She makes love and watches herself from above, emotionally absent. One even tells her, gently, "I feel like you are not here."

She smiles and says, "I am just tired."

She is tired.

Not from work. From the ache she cannot name.

It creeps in around dusk—when the sun paints the windows gold and everything feels too tender. She lies awake at night staring at the ceiling, pulse quickening for no reason. Sometimes, she dreams. Sometimes, she wakes breathless, reaching for water, certain someone has called her name.

One night she dreams of a forest.

Someone is playing a tune she has never heard, yet knows by heart. She follows the sound and sees a figure hunched over the keys—Leo. Only, his back is turned. When he finally faces her, his eyes are bleeding.

She wakes up with a gasp.

She does not sleep again that night.

And the dreams keep coming.

Sometimes he is in the water, reaching out. Sometimes she is bleeding and he is holding her wrists, saying: "Why did you let me go?"

She does not believe in soul connections. That is ridiculous.

But it starts to feel like...he is inside her head.

She stops eating well. Coffee becomes a meal. There are tremors when she stands too long. Dizziness comes in waves. She collapses once in a bookstore and lies to the clerk, says it is just low blood pressure.

Her colleagues tell her to take a break. She nods but does not.

She wins another award. Someone hands her a bouquet and says, "You must be so happy."

She smiles.

But in the photograph taken that night, her eyes look haunted.

She does not speak of him.

To anyone.

But his name lives at the back of her throat. Like something half-swallowed. She is furious with him. How dare he vanish? After everything—after—

She can still remember the exact feel of his breath on her collarbone. The way he held her. They way she poured out her hurt and he listened. The way her worries and anxieties vanished with a simple embrace.

Lies.

He left.

So she tells herself she is just disturbed. Not traumatised. Disturbed, because she was foolish enough to let someone in.

She repeats it like gospel: *I was the hurricane. I left. He just chose to never look back.*

But that tune. That damn tune. It haunts her. Sometimes she hums it under her breath and does not even comprehend.

XXIV

The Softness After Storms

Against every warning, every textbook rule, and every inch of logic that Leo had once clung to, he finds himself drawn to Sylvia—not with the fervour of obsession, but the hush of surrender.

By the time their paths start to bend closer in a way neither of them can ignore. One day, she carefully says, "If anything at all happens between us, I want it to happen when it is not about healing. When it is about choosing."

He nods. The word choosing tastes foreign in his mouth. He has never chosen gently. Never been chosen gently.

They do not begin with declarations or sudden kisses. They begin with long walks. With texts that feel like sunlight after fog. With shared silences that are not uncomfortable, only full. They sit in cafes and libraries. She lends him books. He sends her his favourite songs. Neither of them ever says what this is.

For months, he waits for something to go wrong.

He waits for her to leave.

He waits for the sharp turn, the shattered glass, or the sudden vanishing act.

But Sylvia is not Elise.

Sylvia does not arrive like thunder. She does not make him feel drunk on her presence or starved in her absence. She is calm water. Healing. Steady. A garden that does not demand attention, but flourishes all the same.

He is terrified of that steadiness. He has spent so long surviving in storms that peace feels unnatural, like a trick.

But Sylvia is patient with that fear. One evening, when he tells her, "I am still afraid I will mess this up," she simply replies, "Then we will take it slow enough that you do not."

She sees him. Not the broken parts or the man who lost things. She sees the present-tense version of him. The Leo who is trying. Who still sometimes wakes up from dreams he cannot explain.

There are no fireworks when they finally kiss.

Just warmth.

And then, the exhale.

He does not tell Sylvia that her touch makes his skin remember safety, not chaos. That he once was so emotionally entangled with someone who made him feel like a cathedral falling apart. That Sylivia, instead of mirroring him, mends him—brick by patient brick—restoring the parts he never knew were broken.

He does not need to say it.

She already knows.

They move carefully—because Sylvia is still water, but Leo is still learning not to drown. He is still afraid of breaking her, of being too much, too loud, too full of ghosts.

But Sylvia, in her stillness, teaches him the thing Elise never could.

Love does not have to hurt to be real.

XXV
Woman in the Mirror

It happens on a grey morning with no thunder, no epiphany—only stillness.

The kind of morning where even the air feels suspended, as if waiting for something unnamed to fall apart or come together.

Elise opens Leo's journal.

She does not even remember when she had tucked it away. Perhaps in a fit of anger. Perhaps in one of those feverish nights when dreams clung to her like wet clothing—heavy, intimate, unwelcome.

But it is here now, heavy with dust, humming with a presence.

The first few entries are almost innocent.

Messy handwriting. Half-formed thoughts. Leo at thirteen, scribbling about film scores and rain on the windowpane. There is a note about a dream where he played a grand piano in a burning theatre—before he had even properly learned to play.

Then, as the years pass, the voice matures. Gets quieter. Sharper.

The chaos of adolescence bleeds into the ache of becoming. His words turn inward—reflective, self-critical. There is a season where every entry is just one sentence: "*I do not know how to exist in this skin.*"

There are passages about his father. About silence. About not knowing how to speak until music did it for him.

And then, she notices it, Elise is everywhere.

In the shift of his metaphors. In the way his handwriting suddenly becomes neater, like he wanted to impress even the page.

She is in the way he writes about warmth like it is a borrowed thing. About laughter like he forgot it could belong to him.

She reads an entry: "*Today, Else asked if I believed in fate. I wanted to say yes. I wanted to say her name like a prayer. But I said no. Because I did not want to scare her away with the truth of how deeply I already feel this.*"

And then the later pages—scattered, fraying at the edges.

Elise finds herself in the cracks.

The heartbreak is not theatrical; it is exhausted. Bone-deep. He writes about spirals—those long nights when he could not breathe right. About wanting to disappear into forests, into keys, into anything that was not his own mind.

There is an entry from his early twenties: "*She once said I vanish when the world gets loud. She is right. I do not know how to stay when I am burning. I just want to run.*"

Another: "*I thought love would heal me. But maybe it just uncovered the places that never learned how to hold anything fragile.*"

Elise reads in silence, hunched over the pages like she is holding a relic from another life.

His voice is quiet, restrained. But beneath it, she feels the ache that once tethered them—stretched between two cities, two lives that never managed to breathe in the same rhythm.

And then she finds it—folded neatly in the back, the letter.

The same note he had given her years ago—raw and unedited. Unfiltered Leo. The one who once believed in impossible things.

She does not cry.

She just stares at the page, her fingers trembling as they trace the words like they might collapse if she lets go.

The ache is not sharp. It is dull, slow-burning. Like embers that refuse to die out. It wraps around her chest and sits there like an old friend who never stopped visiting.

That night, she drinks.

Not much. Just enough to take the edge off. To blur the lines between memory and now. To feel something softer than sorrow.

She scrolls through her phone. Finds Leo's name—still greyed out.

Blocked.

After all this time.

She stares at it for a long while, her thumb hovering.

And in her wine-soaked bravery, she tries anyway.

One ring. Then another.

And then the curt mechanical voice:

"The person you are trying to reach is not available."

Something strange happens.

She does not throw the phone. She does not curse or weep.

Instead, a long, cold clarity settles into her bones.

He is gone.
Really gone.

She had pushed him away. Or, he had decided to disappear himself.

And maybe... maybe whatever it is, it is okay.

Because somewhere between chasing closure and avoiding mirrors, she had forgotten something essential: herself.

The girl who once sat under trees sketching rooftops and imagined lives inside them.

The woman who built beauty from silence.

The artist.

The dreamer.

The survivor.

She looks at her reflection in the dark glass of the window. Her own eyes meet her. Tired. Wise. Still burning.

And for the first time in years, she whispers,

"Why do I need anyone?"

At first, it feels defiant. Liberating.

But a second later, the question rings again—softer, lonelier.

"Why do I need anyone?"

She is not sure if she is asking the universe or accusing herself.

Because truthfully, she still wants someone to understand the shadows.

To sit beside her in silence and not flinch.

But maybe needing someone is not the same as needing him.

And the silence, for once, does not echo back with sorrow.

It answers with peace.

Or something close.

The next morning, she wakes up with a decision—not desperate, not reactionary, but clear.

She finds a listing in a quiet countryside village she visited once when she was younger.

Somewhere with ivy on stone walls. A crooked chimney. A garden that begs for wildflowers.

A fireplace that might someday warm more than the room.

She books it.

Packs lightly.

Sketchbooks. A few clothes. The journal. A wind-chime she once bought but never hung.

She does not tell anyone, except her assistant at work and her elderly neighbour who waters her plants.

She does not owe the world an explanation.

This is not running away.

This is returning.

To herself.

To the woman in the mirror.

To the part of her that still believes in something quiet and beautiful, just beyond the ache.

XXVI

The Quiet Where She Waits

Kestren Hollow is not on most maps. The road into it narrows until the world feels stitched together by hedgerows and sky. Sheep cross without urgency. Church bells chime at odd hours. And every ivy-clad cottage has its own garden gate with a name carved in wood.

Elise chooses one that faces the hills—an old stone dwelling with a mossy roof and an iron stove that sighs in winter. The previous owner called it Foxden Cottage. She keeps the name.

It suits her somehow—half-wild, half-tamed.

She plants tulips near the entrance. Lavender beneath the windows. Vines creep up the stone walls as if trying to listen in. A tangle of brambles behind the house hides an old swing, which she clears slowly, reverently. She begins building a vegetable patch, though she knows very little. It does not matter. The hands in soil teach her things books never could.

There are days she speaks to no one.

And for the first time in her life—she is not lonely.

She teaches twice a week at the village school. Art for the little ones. Architecture appreciation for the older ones. Children bring her wildflowers and poorly folded sketches. They do not know about her awards or heartbreaks. They only know her as Miss Marlowe, who draws rooftops and feeds birds.

She sleeps by birdsong, wakes with the light.

No alarms. No screens.

Just the occasional sound of her dogs barking from the front gate.

Yes—the dogs.

They come into her life on a rainy Tuesday, two months after she moves in. A neighbour's friend is rehoming a pair from a nearby farm. Elise only meant to "meet" them, but the moment they bounded toward her—so full of life and contradiction—something unlocked.

The elder is a red-coated Welsh Sheepdog, lean and sharp-eyed. Wary of strangers but fiercely loyal. She names her Branwen, after the mythic heroine.

The younger is a feisty Lakeland Terrier, native to the northern fells. Spirited, bold, and hopelessly cheeky. She calls him Thistle.

Branwen watches the world like it is a test.

Thistle dives into everything like it is a game.

They mirror Elise in ways she had not expected—her caution, her fire, her refusal to be caged.

They sleep by her side. Follow her to the village post. Guard her silence without question.

She stops trying to explain herself.

No one here calls her "intense" or "too much." She is not the sharp girl from university, nor the storm of her twenties. She is just a woman in boots with paint on her hands and stories in her eyes.

She does not dream of Leo anymore.

Or maybe she does—but not in the loud, feverish way of before.

Now, his face floats by gently, like a boat on still water. A smile without ache. A memory without thorns.

She spends her hours painting, reading, and sketching.

She talks to herself. To the wind. To the dogs.

She begins to build something quiet. Something clean.

She doe not call it healing.

She does not call it waiting.

But every time she walks the path behind her cottage, down to the edge of the moor where the wind carries stories, she turns her face toward the horizon, just for a moment—

—and listens.

Not for a name.

Just... a feeling.

Something only she would recognise.

XXVII

That Email Before the Vows

Elise is not expecting anything that morning.

It is raining outside Kestren Hollow—light, polite English rain. She is halfway through a lesson plan for the children when the email arrives. A name she has not seen in years appears in her inbox like a ghost knocking.

Subject: For You, Before I Say I Do

She stares at it.

Her first instinct is to delete it. Second—to read it out of sheer habit, to punish herself.

But something in her still fingers the edges of what they once were. The way you might touch a cracked mug you still cannot throw away.

Her hands tremble as she clicks open.

"Elise,

I do not know if you will read this. I won't lie—I almost did not send it. But I need to say goodbye in the only way I know how. In written words. You always believed in the power of them, did not you?

Attached is the wedding invitation. Sylvia and I are getting married next month. It is in Riversley, nothing grand. Just a quiet ceremony with friends and family.

I thought you would want to know. Or maybe I just needed to tell you.

Well...

There is something you never saw, Elise.

What we were—what we are—was never just love. It was something beyond it. Love has a beginning and an end. You and I... we were more than that. We were twin flames. Two halves that mirrored, that burned too brightly to stay in the same room for long.

You brought out the softness in me. The part of me that wanted to be held. Not admired. Not feared. Just held. I, in turn, drew out your storm. The parts you buried. The wildness you never gave a name.

That is why the dreams kept coming. Why I woke up gasping your name months after you left. Why, I suspect, you did too. We have always been tethered, even when we tried to sever it.

But here is the truth, and it is the hardest one I have had to live with:

You did not recognise it.

Not in time.

Maybe, one day you will.

But I cannot wait anymore, Elise.

Not because I stopped loving you—God knows I tried—but because loving you, hoping for you, started to tear at the fabric of my sanity. You were the hurricane I kept walking into, thinking I could survive it better each time. But I nearly did not, remember?

I had to choose something that did not feel like dying every time I touched it.

Sylvia is a quiet love. Healing love. Not the kind that forces me to write poems in blood, but the kind that wraps bandages with steady hands. I have learned to want that now.

Still—

Even when I will stand beside Sylvia and say "I do," I know a piece of me will still be listening to piano notes drifting through the wind.

We may never meet again. But I believe, with everything I am, that in some other life—somewhere beyond time—you and I are walking hand-in-hand by the sea. Building a crooked little house. Laughing over burnt toast. Making love without fear.

And in that life, you did not run. Me neither.

In that life, I did not have to let go.

Goodbye, Els.

And thank you—for the ache of beautiful things.

—Leo"

She reads it once.

Then again.

Then once more, as if repetition might somehow soften the blow.

A wedding announcement.

From him.

Leo.

No preamble. No warning. Just an email with a quiet subject line and a polite tone.

Her hands go cold first. Then her chest tightens, breath shallow.

She stares at the screen, unblinking, like the words might rearrange themselves. That maybe she read it wrong.

But no—his name is there. Sylvia's name. The date. The words on the attached invite: *"We hope you can send your warm wishes."* She almost laughs. Warm wishes? She is still trying to cauterize wounds he left open.

Her blood starts to buzz. Heat rises under her skin like a storm breaking surface. The peace she had gathered in the countryside in all this time shatters.
How dare he.
After everything.

She paces. Her jaw clenches.
She opens her contacts and stares at his name.

Her thumb hovers over the call button.

She does not plan what she will say. She does not need to.
This is not the kind of pain that simmers. It erupts.

And then—
She taps *"Call."*

It rings.

Oh, so he has finally unblocked me, she thinks, blood buzzing. How noble. Probably expecting a graceful congratulations, a sweet little *"I am so happy for you."*

He picks up.

"Elise?"

Her voice comes sharp, like a blade unsheathed. "How dare you."

Leo exhales, already bracing. "Elise, I—"

"No," she snaps. "You do not get to Elise me right now. You do not get that luxury."

She is pacing now, her voice rising like a storm surge. "You vanish from my life—completely disappear—and then send me a wedding announcement like it is a bloody newsletter?"

He winces.

"Who is she?"

"Els..."

"No. Do not Els me either. Who is she, Leo?"

A pause.

"She is Sylvia...My former therapist," he says, low.

There is a beat. Just enough for her fury to gather and sharpen.

"Oh," Elise says, dangerously calm. "A therapist. How poetic. So you picked someone trained to fix people. What was I then? A case study? A practice run?"

Leo closes his eyes. He knows her rage is not about Sylvia. Not really.

"I see it now," she spits. "You wanted peace. Stability. The kind of woman who does not make you feel too much. Calm dinners, soft voices, a curated little life with breathing techniques and silence that does not scare you."

She laughs, bitter and breathless. "And I was the chaos you had to recover from. The fire you had to extinguish. I bet she never yells. I bet she never makes you want to throw your phone against a wall. I bet she never makes you feel like you are drowning."

"Elise, it is not—"

"You made me feel like I was hard to love," she cuts in, her voice cracking now. "That my fire, my confusion, my truth—was inconvenient."

He tries to say something, anything, but she barrels on:

"You called me your twin flame in that email, remember that? Let us go there. Even though I do not believe in that crap. Never have. But you—you threw around words like that like they meant something. Maybe that is the thing about flames—they burn. And maybe you just got tired of the smoke."

Her words sting, not because they are unfair—but because they are true in ways he cannot argue with.

"But I remember everything," she says, her voice quieter now, but no less venomous. "Every time you ghosted me. Every door you closed. Every silence that felt like punishment."

She laughs again—harsh, unhinged.

"You want to know what is hilarious? You with a therapist. Of course. After me, you needed stability. A live-in emotional first-aid kit. And what do I get? An email. That is my closure. That is my ending."

"Elise..."

"No. Do not say my name like it still means something to you."

A silence stretches.

"I hope she fixes you," she says finally, cold and trembling. "Because I could not. Or maybe I was not broken in the right way. Not soft enough. Not scared enough. You did not want love, Leo. You wanted peace. You wanted someone who would never hold a mirror to you."

Then, flatly:

"Have a happy life."

Click.

The line goes dead.

Silence.

He stands there for a long time, the phone still at his ear like it might bring her back.

Then—

He sighs.

Of course. Elise. Fiery, volatile, unforgettable. She was still the same. And he... he was not.

She would never realise. Never see what it cost him to let go.

He walks to his closet. Pulls open the door with mechanical calm. Inside, buried beneath folded jumpers and dust, is the shirt she wore that day. The morning light still caught in her hair. That half-smile still floating in his memory like smoke.

He lifts the shirt to his face. Breathes in.

It does not smell like her anymore.

And just like that, something within him folds.

Maybe he had done the right thing.

Or maybe...

Maybe he had pushed her into a well she would never climb out from.

Maybe he had been too consumed with protecting himself to ever try calming her fire.

He knew her. Did not he? Knew that behind that anger was a woman who had once stood on rooftops and trusted him with her heart.

What if someone else comes along now and... extinguishes it? That wildness. That fierce, burning part of her that scared him and seduced him all at once?

But how could he protect it and protect himself?

He could not. Not anymore.

His mind is tired. His body, worn.

Elise is unpredictable. And his sanity is a thread he cannot afford to fray.

He closes the closet. Locks it.

Sylvia is peace.

He whispers it to himself like a mantra.

Then, he reaches for the drawer and pulls out the bottle Sylvia gave him.

Just one pill. An SOS.

He swallows it dry.

And lets the silence wrap around him like a soft, sterile blanket.

Outside, the wind rustles leaves.

Inside, nothing moves.

XXVIII

The Realisation Was Always There

She slams the phone down, breathless.

Not crying. Not screaming. Just winded—like someone had punched the air out of her lungs and left her standing in the wreckage.

Her heart gallops. Her hands are clenched, nails biting into skin. Her jaw aches from how tightly it is set.
The words she just flung at him still echo in the room. Loud. Ugly. True.

She is pacing again, like a caged thing. The anger is a storm, crackling through her ribs, rushing to her throat. She opens her mouth—no sound. Just the sound of her breath. Shallow. Unsteady.

Damn it, Leo.

How dare he. How dare he just write to her with that calm detachment, that careful tenderness wrapped in closure. And how dare she...care.

She drops into the chair. She simply sits there—frozen in that moment between breath and grief—as the cursor blinks on the screen, waiting, indifferent.

Outside, the rain has softened. The hills are wrapped in mist. Her tea has gone cold. But Elise does not move. Her eyes trace Leo's words over and over until they no longer feel like letters, but bruises pressed into her skin.

Twin flames.

Storm and softness.

The house they never built.

The ache in her chest is not just regret—it is recognition. Like hearing a melody you have known since birth but forgot you knew.

That night, she lies awake. The email open on her phone beside her, glowing faintly in the dark. She does not read it again. She does not need to.

Because she finally understands what she had always known and never allowed herself to say and accept.

It was him.

It had always been Leo.

She thinks back.

To the dreams.

The ones she had dismissed. The ones she had blamed on stress, on her collapsing appetite, on her messed-up sleeping patterns. The ones where shs had woken up in a sweat, heart hammering, convinced someone was falling—he was falling.

Then, there were the dreams from when they were younger. Strange, fragmented flickers. Once, she dreamt of fire licking piano keys. Another time, she was sketching a house with no doors, only to find Leo standing inside it, looking lost.

Back then, she laughed them off.

Just vivid nonsense, she told herself. An overstimulated brain.

But now, they shimmer in her memory like messages she had ignored.

As if some ancient part of her always knew. Had been trying to tell her something long before her conscious mind caught up.

Why had not she listened?

Was it pride? Ego? Her own damn walls? Or those shreds of mistrust that had accumulated over the years?

Because if he had cared, he would not have blocked me.

But oh—had not she felt something?

A dull weight in her chest, weeks before the email.

A familiar stillness that made her stomach tighten for no reason.

A restlessness that came from a ghost she could not name.

To call him. To shake him. To scream.

To force him to feel what she felt.

But she had not. She had worn her pain like a crown. She had clung to anger like righteousness.

And now—now it was too late.

Leo had found peace. Built a world where she no longer fit.

He would be marrying someone who helped him put himself back together.

And he had written to her not for hope. But for release.

The worst part was not that he was gone.

It was that he had always been there—quiet, waiting—and she had not seen him.

She had not seen him.

Not really. Not past her own longing.

She was so consumed with wanting to be chosen, she forgot

he was breaking too. Quietly. Delicately. In ways that never made it into words.

And then the thought hits her, sharp and sudden:

He nearly died, Elise.

She sits bolt upright, stomach hollowing.

He did not say it—not directly. But it was there, unspoken. Tucked between sentences.

"I had to choose something that did not feel like dying every time I touched it."

She feels sick.

She gets up. Walks barefoot through the dark house, her breath shallow. The walls hum with memories. And Leo is everywhere now—

In the unfinished sketch by the window.

In the song she hums without knowing.

In the words she never dared write down.

He mocks her, tender and cruel in her own voice:

"I was that shadow behind every failed attempt at love.

The reason no other man stayed.

Why every kiss felt counterfeit."

Yes. He had never left.

He was the unanswered question.

The haunting.

The echo.

And now she sees it clearly—he was the only one she ever truly gave herself to. And she gave him nothing soft. Nothing easy. Just fire, expectation, and absence.

The next morning, she does not cry.

She wraps a shawl around her shoulders and steps onto the porch.

The air is cold, crisp with early light.

The hills roll gently under pale clouds.

A dog barks in the distance. A child laughs.

And Elise exhales, her breath fogging the dawn.

The ache is still there. But it no longer chokes her.

She touches her heart. Whispers—not in longing, not in pain, but in peace:

"Leo, you will always be with me—deep within the beats of my heart."

A name like a prayer.

A name like surrender.

A name like coming home.

XXIX

The Life He Did Not Choose

Leo is in his early thirties when he marries.

It is a small wedding—just a few friends, family, and a garden full of late summer roses. No grand declarations. No drama. Just sunlight, vows whispered like old poems, and the feeling that maybe—just maybe—peace is possible.

Sylvia wears her hair up. Her eyes are clear. She does not ask for forever. Only presence. And Leo, who once bled for every *what if,* now finds relief in the quiet certainty of her love.

Two years of courtship. A slow thawing. A shared rhythm.

Then came the children.

Two of them. Bright, curious, and nothing like the ghosts he once carried. They wake him with laughter. Cling to his sleeves. Say "Papa" like it is the safest word in the world.

He learns to make lunches.

He learns to be soft.

He learns to live without looking over his shoulder.

His life stabilises—not just in routine, but in heart. The wild ache that once made him feel alive now seems... distant. Like a fever long broken.

He does not speak of Elise yet.

Not to Sylvia. Not even in the dark.

But some nights, when the house sleeps, he creeps downstairs and lifts the cover off his piano.

He has started again.

Not with the wild abandon of his youth, but with patience. Reverence. A kind of grief woven into every note.

There is one tune he always comes back to.

It begins with a jagged left hand—low, fractured chords. Then rises into a melody that feels like wind threading through trees. It is chaotic. Yearning. Unfinished.

He never wrote it for Sylvia.

He never even finishes it.

Always—always—he stops halfway, right before the bridge. As if the memory tucked into the next few bars is one he cannot quite bear to touch.

Sylvia never asks. But she hears it.

Once, she says, "There is someone in that song, is not there?"

He does not lie. But he does not answer.

Instead, he holds her. Long and quiet.

He is grateful for this life. Truly. There is warmth in it. Laughter. Healing. He wants this—this stillness—not the madness Elise brought in like a tide.

And yet...

Sometimes, when he is out walking with the children—one on his shoulders, the other chasing butterflies—he will glance at a stranger in the distance. A woman with dark hair. Or a figure standing still on a bridge.

For a second, just a flicker—
His breath stutters.
But it is never her.
And then the moment passes. Always.
There is no tragedy here. No betrayal.
Just...the life he did not *choose*.

XXX

Children of Other Lives

Years pass.

Slowly at first, then all at once—like seasons changing when you are not looking.

The house is full of light that afternoon—golden slants filtering through gauzy curtains, warming the oak floors, dust motes dancing like tiny spirits. Somewhere, soup simmers. A child's book lies open on the couch. The calm, domestic kind of day.

Leo's daughter sits at the piano.

She is only six, but curious fingers run with an elegance far beyond her years. She hums when she plays, always just under her breath, like she is speaking a language she does not yet understand. He had not taught her much—just scales, a few nursery rhymes. And yet here she is.

Her small hands find a series of notes.

Low... low... high... dissonant.

Leo freezes.

The tune rises—wild, broken keys, a half-remembered melody that lives deep in his spine. That song. That song.

The one he never finished. The one that was never written down. The one born from longing and loss and everything he tried to leave behind.

And she plays it—not perfectly, but with enough resemblance to shake the air.

He does not breathe.

Across the room, Sylvia looks up from a book. "You okay?"

He startles slightly. Then forces a smile.

"Yeah," he says. "Just an old memory."

But something in him won't settle.

How could she know?

The only place those notes ever existed was in his mind. And in Elise. And at night when everyone would sleep.

He watches his daughter's hands, small and sure, echo a song birthed in heartbreak. It feels like someone—something—has reached across the veil of time to remind him: some connections do not die. They pass through the cracks. Through blood. Through spirit.

A quiet ache spreads in his chest.

Later that night, after the children are asleep, he sits alone at the piano. He tries to play it again.

It comes out unfamiliar.

Too polished. Too neat.

It had always belonged to that part of him that Elise touched. The untamed part. The part that still flickered, somewhere, even now.

He closes the lid.

In the silence, the ghost of a note lingers. Half-formed. Barely there.

Children of other lives, he thinks.

Of course they will carry echoes.

XXXI

Kestren Hollow Cafe

After a couple of months, they plan a quiet weekend away—a small family trip to the hills, nothing extravagant. Just time to breathe, to be.

Leo had mapped it all out a few days before, neatly folding routes and weather updates into the glovebox. A familiar road, a few favourite stops, maybe a picnic if the children behave.

They are supposed to be heading further up the hills. But Leo suggests they take a short detour, so the kids can stretch their legs, and Sylvia can get a strong coffee. The morning mist has just begun to lift, curling like silver ribbon across the fields. The roads wind narrow and sleepy through stone-fenced lanes and scattered sheep.

Kestren Hollow appears like something imagined—and a quietness settles over the car, not empty but full—of memory, of something unspoken. Even the children fall silent, as if the village has asked them to listen.

They park near a low-built cafe at the village edge. The sign reads The Hollow Mug—painted by hand, faded at the corners.

Leo offers to go inside alone.

The bell above the door rings as he enters.

The scent hits first—fresh bread, herbs, something faintly like lavender. It is warm inside, sunlight slanting through paned windows and catching on polished wood. There is music playing faintly—a violin sonata, maybe, or a piano piece he once knew.

He steps up to the counter.

And freezes.

Behind it stands Elise.

Older, yes. But time has only burnished her. Her hair, longer now, tied loosely. Laugh lines curve her face gently, but her eyes—God, her eyes—are the same.

For a moment, she does not see him. She is scribbling on a paper napkin absently, in that same left-handed tilt.

Then she looks up.

And time forgets how to move.

Leo forgets to breathe.

Elise goes still. The pen slips from her hand and rolls to the floor. Her lips part, but no sound comes. They just... look.

Not with shock.

Not even sorrow.

But a stunned recognition. As if a story they both buried had walked into the room.

He looks older too—more weathered than she remembers. There is grey at his temples, lines near his mouth. But it suits him. He has softened at the edges. Less boy, more man. A man who has lived through silence, like she has.

Neither of them moves.

For once, there are no ghosts between them.

Only two people who once dreamt together, now standing in the warmth of a morning years too late.

The woman behind Elise—perhaps a helper—pokes her head in. "Els, someone at table four wants the honey scones."

Elise blinks. "Right—yes."

She bends, picks up her pen, smooths the napkin flat.

Leo swallows.

"I will just get a flat white," he says, voice steadier than he feels.

She nods once. "Of course."

As she turns to the espresso machine, he exhales, hands trembling slightly, and takes a long look at her.

She is not shaking. She is not flustered.

She is still Elise—but quieter now. As if she no longer creates chaos with words and sketches. As if the ache has gentled into something almost beautiful.

He wonders if she dreams of him still.

He wonders what might have been.

But he does not speak.

Not yet.

He takes the coffee when she passes it to him. Their fingers brush, lightly. Not long enough to say anything. Just enough to feel that nothing—nothing—has truly disappeared.

Outside, his daughter runs around the car, laughing. Sylvia waves.

And inside, Elise watches him go.

XXXII
Small Conversations

Sylvia waves from the passenger seat, smiling at the familiar gleam in Leo's eyes—until it lingers too long, too still, too quiet.

She watches through the windshield as he turns to the cafe door again. He has not moved in a while.

Sylvia's smile fades a little. She had always known there was someone. Never a name. Never a story. But a presence. A shadow stitched into the folds of Leo's midnight music, in the silence that followed that song he could not finish.

And now, watching him freeze in the sunlight like that, she knows.

She gets out of the car.

"The kids want cake," she says, voice easy. "You mind getting them something?"

Leo's eyes flick to her, then back at the cafe. "Yeah. Sure."

"I will come too."

Inside, the bell rings again. Elise looks up.

She was not expecting more.

She definitely was not expecting all of them.

Leo walks in first, his face unreadable. Behind him, a girl around six bounds in, her curls bouncing, eyes wide with curiosity. A boy a few years younger ambles in behind, grinning as he surveys the cakes on display.

And then—Sylvia.

Graceful. Steady. There is nothing confrontational in her. Just observation. Quiet intelligence. And a slight, almost imperceptible tightening of her expression as her eyes fall on Elise.

The air shifts. Subtly.

Elise smiles first. "Back again already?"

"The kids could not resist," Leo says.

"I do not blame them," Elise murmurs, turning to the girl. "What is your name?"

"Elsa," the girl says brightly.

Elise's heart gives one hard thud—but she says nothing. Of course.

"And I am Jonah," the boy adds, already pressed against the glass, evaluating the options like a connoisseur.

"They are beautiful," Elise says. Her voice is steady. Smooth as porcelain. "You have done well."

Leo nods once. "Thanks."

Sylvia steps forward. "I am Sylvia. I think...I think you and Leo knew each other once?"

Elise turns to her, and for the first time, their eyes truly meet. Two women with nothing and everything between them.

"Yes," Elise replies gently. "A long time ago."

Something flickers across Sylvia's face. Curiosity. Caution. And something like understanding. She does not press.

"You have a lovely place," Sylvia says. "Charming little hamlet."

"Thank you," Elise says, softer now. "It is home."

They order cake—carrot, lemon drizzle, something chocolate for Elsa.

They sit at the window table. Talk drifts—harmless, neutral. The weather. The view from the hills. A story about Jonah falling into a stream last summer. Elise laughs lightly at all the right places. Smiles when Elsa tells her she wants to be a pianist and a vet. Her eyes linger only briefly on Leo when he is not looking.

Inside her, something crumbles. The children are beautiful. Sylvia is kind. And Leo...

Leo watches her with the eyes of someone who still remembers her voice in the dark.

But he does not say her name.

She does not say his either.

The cake is served. Tea is poured. Sunlight filters through the lace curtains, turning everything golden and suspended, like a moment caught in amber.

When they get up to leave, Elise walks them to the door.

"It was really lovely meeting you," Sylvia says. And Elise knows she means it. Not as competition. Not as territory. But as a woman who saw something and chose stillness instead of war.

Elise nods. "Take care of them."

Sylvia smiles faintly. "I do. I will."

The bell chimes as they exit. Jonah runs ahead. Elsa clutches her father's hand, swinging it.

Leo is the last to leave.

He looks at Elise once more.

No words.

Just that look—that impossible, eternal, devastating look.

Then he turns.

And she watches him walk away again, this time with children laughing and a woman who did not lose him.

XXXIII
Waterfall

Elise watches him walk down the path, Elsa's small hand tucked in his, Sylvia's arm brushing gently against his shoulder. The sun filters through the trees, and for one fragile moment, the world looks like a photograph she was never meant to be in.

She holds herself still.

Every breath a discipline.

Every muscle, a tightrope.

But when the bell above the cafe door chimes with his final step away—when the echo of that sound fades into silence—her chest caves in.

The sound that escapes her is not a sob. Not at first.
It is the sound of a held breath finally giving up.

She sinks behind the counter. Her knees hit the floor with a thud.
And then, like a dam breached, the tears come.

Sudden.
Unstoppable.
Ferocious.

She buries her face into her palms as her shoulders shake, salt stinging her skin. No grace in it. No composure. It is not the weeping of a heartbroken woman—it is the collapse of years. Of what-if's, of dreams denied, of every moment she swallowed instead of speaking.

The ache claws upward, years too late.

She cries for the boy who played the piano in the dark and waited for her to listen.

She cries for the girl who thought time would always wait.

She cries because she has nothing left to hold onto—not even anger.

And for the first time in forever, the grief does not feel noble or poetic.

It feels stupid. Ugly. Unforgivable.

She rests her forehead on the cool tile. Her dogs come to her—one resting his head on her thigh, the other curling beside her feet, silent witnesses to her undoing.

The afternoon moves on around her.

Outside, birds call. Leaves rustle. The world does not pause for heartbreak.

But inside this small cafe in Kestren Hollow, a woman finally breaks.

And somewhere in her, something else breaks free.

Not hope.

Not love.

But a surrender. A relinquishing of the need to rewrite what has already been carved in stone.

When she finally rises, her face is swollen, her voice silent, but her body lighter.

She walks to the back, washes her hands.

Washes her face.

Washes the day off her skin.

Then she pours herself a cup of tea and carries it out to the garden behind the cafe—ajdacent to her own house. Her dogs follow.

And she sits beneath the elder tree as twilight drapes itself over the hills, watching the steam curl from her cup as if her pain could leave her that gently too.

XXXIV

The Last Page

That night, Kestren Hollow is hushed under a cobalt sky. The air is cool, touched with woodsmoke. Elise sits by the window, a flickering candle the only light in the room. Its flame dances with the wind that seeps through the cracks, steady and wavering all at once—just like her.

She is wrapped in an old cardigan, sleeves pushed past her elbows, a mug of tea gone cold at her side. Her dogs sleep curled at her feet, their breathing soft, grounding.

On her lap lies Leo's journal.

She has not opened it since that night before leaving for Kresten.

Tonight, she does.

The familiar scrawl greets her, ink faded even more with time. She turns the pages slowly, not searching anymore. Not bleeding, either. Just reading. Remembering. The tenderness in his words. The rage. The longing. The confusion. The thread of her woven through every thought.

There is nothing left to discover. No hidden message. No secret hope.

And still—
still—
her hands tremble when she reaches the final pages, still blank, waiting.

The candle flickers once, casting gold across the paper.

Elise picks up a pen.

She does not hesitate this time.

Her handwriting is firm, slanted, the pressure just enough to leave an indent.

"Some people are not meant to be ours.
They are mirrors—so we remember who we were, and what we lost by not looking."

She stares at the words for a long moment. Then, slowly, she closes the journal.

Closes it for good.

It does not feel like an ending.

It feels like a reckoning.

She places it back on the shelf—not buried, not displayed. Just...there. A chapter that once mattered. A reflection that once burned.

Elise blows out the candle. Darkness folds gently around her.

She walks to the bedroom, the dogs padding after her.

She will sleep tonight. Not because she is healed. Not because she is free.

But because there is nothing more to chase.

Some stories do not end with answers.

Some just end.

XXXV
Footnotes

The years drift like pages caught in wind. Seasons fold into each other—autumns of rust, winters of hush, springs of pale hope.

Leo's life moves forward. A steady rhythm.

His children grow. Elsa composes now, fingers dancing over ivory keys the way his once did. He teaches her to listen, not just play—to feel the pauses between notes. That is where the truth lives.

He still laughs with Sylvia. They garden together, fight over toast crumbs, hold hands during movies. It is a quiet, sturdy kind of love. Something earned. Something that stays.

But on some nights, when the world dims and the house settles into sleep, Leo sits by the window. The same tune—wild, broken, and half-done—returns to his fingers. He never plays it for long. Just enough to feel her ghost.

Not the young Elise who once ran barefoot across dewy fields.

But the woman in the cafe. Wiser. Radiant. Silent.
The one who said nothing, but looked like she remembered

everything.

Part of him—maybe the truest part—is still buried somewhere in those hills.

Far away, in Kestren Hollow, Elise tends to her life.

She plants flowers. Fixes fences. Restores broken garden chairs for neighbours. She teaches village children how to draw trees that do not look the same, skies that are not always blue.

The dogs grow old beside her. Loyal and protective. A quiet pack.

Some evenings, when the breeze shifts, she hears something faint.

A piano.

Or maybe just the ache of memory in the wind.

She does not follow the sound.

She simply listens.

They never meet again.

But somewhere—beneath the soft moss of the years, between ink on a journal's pages and the echo of unfinished melodies—they remain.

Not in the way love stories are written.

But in the way footnotes remember what the story forgot to say.

Epilogue: A House For Two

Elise Marlowe dies peacefully in her fifties, on a quiet morning in early spring.
There is no pain, only stillness.
A cup of tea sits unfinished on the sill. The light filters in gently, touching the edges of her solitude.

The village mourns in the gentle way only small places can. They speak of her stubborn kindness, her sharp eye for broken things, her garden that always seemed to bloom early. They remember how she never raised her voice, but her silence could still fill a room.

Among her things, a kind elderly couple from the village—whom Elise had been almost like a daughter to—find a small, carefully wrapped package tied with string, tucked away in a drawer. Inside is a letter written in Elise's handwriting, requesting it be sent to an address in Weltingham.

She is buried beneath the apple tree she once planted by hand.

Weeks later, on a quiet evening, Leo receives a package with no return address.

Leo, a little more silent around the edges, with his hair flecked with silver. The lines near his eyes have deepened from years of squinting into sunlight, not sadness. His days are simple—mornings with his family, quiet dinners with Sylvia, evening walks where the past trails him like a second shadow.

But when he sees her handwriting on the parcel, he knows.

Not just what it is.
But what it means. He has known it for a while now. In dreams he has endured in silence.

She is gone.

He does not cry. There is no gasp, no crumbling. Just a hush inside him, like the air before the storm. A quiet reverence for something irreplaceable that has left the world.

He opens it gently, as though she might still be watching.

Inside is a sketch—delicate and deliberate. A house, etched in soft charcoal, perched on the edge of a cliff where sea and sky hold each other. Ivy spills down warm stone walls. The windows are wide, catching the light. A single path winds past wild grass and daffodils. And by the hearth, a piano.

It is unmistakably them.

Beneath the sketch, a note.

"If we had been braver, this is what I would have built for us."

—Els

No goodbye. Just that. But it is enough.

Leo presses the paper to his chest and lets the silence wrap around him. It is the same silence he has known for decades—between melodies, between memories, between every word they left unsaid.

He rises and walks to the piano. The house sleeps behind him—Sylvia is out on errands. A clock ticks faintly. He places his hands on the keys.

And plays.

The melody begins in fragments, fragile as frost. Then it grows.

A song that weeps and glows and remembers.
A song with no beginning, no ending—only ache.
Storm and stillness.
Twin flames and torn letters.
And the rhythm of a heart that beat once for her.

As his fingers glide, something shifts.

The music begins to echo the poem he once wrote, long ago, on a nameless beach where she might have stood too—

One word of tenderness

"Sitting by the seashore
On an inky black sky
Studded with diamond stars shining down
And the empowering roar of the waves
Like the arms of a long-lost lover reaching out to you
And the tender wisps of wind kissing
The cascade of that beautiful hair
And the desperate loneliness
Creeping within that palpitating heart
Craving for one word of tenderness"
- Leo

And that is what this music is.
Not closure. Not grief.
But one word of tenderness that came too late, and still

meant everything.

He does not stop playing this time.

The final notes rise—ghostlike, aching—and hang there in the air. Then fall, slowly, like autumn leaves, like years.

A song for the house they never built.

For the ember, she kept glowing.

For the boy who never forgot her.

For the girl who carried him through her chaos.

A house for two.

In music.

In memory.

Forever.